CHRONICLES OF ECHOES

ALVIN DORSEY JR

Table of Content

Chapter 1

The Mysterious Music Box

"Damn it," Alex muttered lowly, letting out a sigh as he stared down at the empty glass in his hand. It was his final drink of the night, a harsh reality considering his near-empty pockets. The idea of asking for a tab crossed his mind, but Melissa, the bartender, had made it abundantly clear that she wouldn't be extending that courtesy to him anymore. Two glasses of whiskey were a meager attempt to drown the deep-seated pain he carried, but it would have to suffice for now.

Leaving a few bills on the counter to cover his drinks, Alex shrugged into his coat and walked out of the bar. As he stepped back onto the rain-soaked streets of Ravenwood, the city, with its gloomy facade and slick pavements, seemed to mirror his own despondent mood. The rhythmic patter of raindrops and the haunting amber glow defined the city's character, quite reminiscent of a ghetto in an otherwise cyberpunk setting - almost as if it was deliberately left behind in time.

As Alex wandered through the streets, maybe trying to find his way back or trying to get lost in the heart of it, the city's whispers morphed in his ears into a chorus, hinting at hidden depths and tales untold. Long stretches of dilapidated buildings loomed overhead on either side, their windows reflected the city's myriad secrets in fractured patterns. Ravenwood was definitely a city with a heartbeat, and tonight, it throbbed with a melancholic rhythm.

Alex knew it was getting late, and he had to head home, but he just couldn't help but wander off for a bit. A shy smile crossed as a faint voice echoed from the back of his mind. "You're like a cat! All you need is a faint smell of fish and you've already lost your way!" his mother used to say, and for the most part, she was right. Considering how often he would cross paths with trouble, it was a surprise Alex's curiosity hadn't yet gotten him killed.

With a rough sense of the direction he was heading in, Alex fastened his pace, acting in accordance to his better judgement to not stay out too late. But it only took a couple of turns for him to find himself lost. Suddenly, as he looked around to find a way out, the realization creeped up on him that he had never been to this part of the city. Having called Ravenwood home since his birth, Alex was absolutely baffled - he was certain that he knew every in and out of this place. And yet, here was a neighborhood that he had never once seen in his life – he was sure of it. Because if he had, he would have certainly remembered such a conspicuous store with a huge neon sign "ANTIQUE" hanging over it.

As his stride progressed, Alex felt his legs grow heavier. He could feel tension all around him as clearly as if he could see it. He stopped for a minute, trying to make sense of what he was feeling. There was no doubt something mysterious and strange about this alley – and it seemed as though it was calling to him.

"Your destiny calls, Alex. You can't escape it," a faint whisper reached back from the back of his ears, prompting him to look over his shoulders, and then all around him, only to find no one by his side. Alex felt like he was going crazy, and he hadn't even had to drink that much tonight! He felt a strong urge to turn back and keep running away. But like a curse, his curiosity had him now gripped. Even as every fiber of being told him to run, there was a strange feeling of familiarity in his mind that made him start walking towards the end of the road where the store stood.

The antique store, bathed in a dim and ethereal light, stood out like a relic from a bygone era. The creaky sign above the door swayed slightly in the cold wind, casting eerie shadows on the wet pavement. The store seemed frozen in time, a haven forgotten treasures and untold stories. A chilly wind blew past as Alex stood for a second in front of the entrance before pushing the door open, jingling a soft chime and revealing a world of ancient artifacts within.

Alex hesitated for a moment, then shook off the eerie sensation and stepped further into the shop. The air within the shop hung heavy, laden with the scent of aging paper and wood polish, an aroma that spoke of centuries passed and secrets kept. This was not just a threshold to a mere shop; it was a portal to a world unseen, a world that starkly contrasted the city's pulsating life outside. With each step, the whispering of the shop's relics grew more insistent, as if they were alive, each item a sentinel of history eager to divulge its tale.

Behind a dusty glass counter stood the shopkeeper, a man probably in his late 50s with silver hair that seemed to shimmer in the soft glow of a flickering lamp. His fancy but obsolete-looking Victorian-era suit made it seem like he had an immaculate fashion sense but from a time long forgotten. His eyes, sharp and piercing, bore into Alex's soul as if reading the very essence of his being.

"Take a look around; just don’t touch anything," said the shopkeeper as he shifted his gaze back to the mechanical toy he was tinkering with in his hands. Alex nodded in acknowledgment, drawn to the myriad of items within the store. Ancient books with worn leather covers, tarnished trinkets with stories etched into their surfaces, and dusty relics from a forgotten past surrounded him.

Suddenly, his tracks stopped as something from the back shelves of the store caught his eye. Alex's gaze was ensnared by a singular object among the shop's antiquities - a diminutive, exquisitely carved music box, strikingly reminiscent of one his grandfather had cherished. This serendipitous discovery sent a cascade of memories crashing over him, vivid recollections of distant lands and ancient times, of enthralling tales steeped in magic and wonder that had first kindled the flames of storytelling within his soul.

The music box, with its intricate designs and air of time-honored secrets, seemed to resonate with a deeper meaning, almost as if the universe itself was reaching out, urging him towards an inevitable path.

“The Box of Echoes,” the shopkeeper’s words echoed inside. “It’s been here for ages, that stupid box. They say that the box chooses its owner, but all I’ve seen it do is send potential customers flying.”

Alex was too engrossed in the box to realize what the shopkeeper said came as words of caution. Before the shopkeeper could say another word, he had already walked up to the cupboard and taken the box out to hold it in his palm. The box, mysteriously warm to the touch, emanated a faint light that danced in the air. In his palm, the carvings on the box glowed up, as if reacting to Alex's touch. His hands trembled slightly as they clung to the enigmatic box, his fingers caressing its surface as if seeking answers from the very material it was made of. In that suspended moment, the cacophony of the shop's ambient sounds faded into a distant, almost forgotten hum, gradually diminishing in significance. The world beyond the shop's confines ceased to exist as if time itself had chosen this moment to slow its relentless march.

The shopkeeper's eyes widened in surprise as he understood the gravity of what he had just witnessed - the box had finally chosen its owner. As the glow enveloped Alex, a strange energy seemed to connect them at that moment.

"I'll take this," said Alex, still captivated by the box's mysterious energies. "That'll be $29.99," the shopkeeper responded.

Standing in front of the counter, Alex emptied his pockets. A wave of disappointment washed over him with the realization that the only money he was left with was a dollar bill and a few cents worth of coins.

"I'm sorry, but this is all I have" – Alex may not have said it out loud, but the shopkeeper read it clearly off his face. With a deep sigh, the keeper looked down at the singular bill and the bundle of coins resting on his counter and said, "Fine! You'll be doing me a favor by taking it anyway. The Box of Echoes has a way of choosing its owner, and tonight, it has chosen you." "Are you sure?" Alex asked, not yet being able to believe the discount he had been given.

"It's been sitting here for years now, not earning me a dime. Might as well take the dollar now than sit regretting later," the shopkeeper said.

"Fair enough," Alex sounded convinced this time. He tucked the box into his jacket pocket and with a nod of departure to the shopkeeper, made his way out of the door. He may have just traded his last remaining money for this box, but somehow, he just felt like everything happened as it was meant to be. This little music box -there was certainly something more to it, and he just couldn't wait to find out.

The rain had stopped, and Alex emerged into the night, the city bathed in the afterglow of the cleansing raindrops, glistening under the celestial tapestry of stars. His pace hastened as he tried to retrace his path back from the antique store, the fragrance of rain still lingering in the air as a subtle reminder of the downpour's recent embrace. He didn’t even think to look back; his only goal was to get home as soon as possible.

Once inside the familiar confines of his apartment, Alex couldn't resist the urge to thoroughly inspect the outer decorations of the music box. Intricate patterns adorned its surface, telling tales of forgotten realms and ancient magics. The carvings seemed to come alive under the soft glow of his apartment's dim lights, revealing a hidden world within the box's enchanted exterior.

Seating himself at the worn-out table, Alex gingerly cradled the music box in his hands. The room pulsated with an ethereal energy, and the air crackled with the promise of something extraordinary. It was a moment suspended in time, a choice that would unveil the depths of the unknown. With bated breath, fueled by an intoxicating blend of curiosity and an uncanny feeling of destiny, Alex decided to unlock the secrets held within the Box of Echoes. He delicately raised the lid of the box, and a low creak followed by a melody, both haunting and enchanting, filled the room. But as captivating as the music was, Alex was left shocked and bewildered within the span of a blink - the comforting walls of his apartment suddenly dissolved into thin air as he realized himself in the middle of a forest.

The abruptness of the shift left him momentarily breathless, struggling to grasp the reality of the transformation. He could feel it in his body - this wasn't the world he was familiar with. The two otherworldly moons softly lighting up his path ahead with their ethereal silver glow in the night sky confirmed his suspicions. He had been uprooted from his realm and catapulted into another, with no explanation and no warnings. And yet, there was a strange sensation inside him that he had either already been here or was meant to be.

The forest reverberated with an orchestra of unfamiliar yet strangely soothing sounds — the rustling of leaves, the distant calls of creatures hidden in the night, and a gentle breeze that bore the hushed murmurs of age-old mysteries. The trees whispered ancient secrets, and the air shimmered with magic. It was a place untouched by time, where reality and fantasy danced in perfect harmony. Alex stood in awe, the music box still in hand, as the forest beckoned him to explore its mysteries.

With a heart pounding in anticipation, Alex decided to walk through the path in the forest and see where it led. As he ventured deeper into the enchanting woods, he could sense other presences around him - animals, birds, and other ethereal creatures flitting between the trees, casting mischievous glances in his direction. The Box of Echoes continued its haunting melody, guiding Alex through this surreal landscape. The ground beneath his feet felt soft, and the air was charged with the scent of unseen flowers. Waves of various emotions washed over him and yet, somehow, amidst all this, Alex found himself at ease like he never had been before in his life.

Minutes turned to hours as his journey continued through the dense forest before the trees finally relented, unveiling a moonlit clearing, and in its heart, stood an enigmatic figure draped in a garment spun from the very fabric of the night sky. As he got closer, Alex almost stopped in his tracks for once as the features of the figure finally began to take clear form for him - there was a beauty of celestial quality standing right in front of him, elegant as, unlike anything he had ever seen in his life.

"Welcome to Echoes," the figure's voice, ancient yet strangely youthful, resonated through the moonlit clearing, sending shivers down Alex's spine. Each word carried an enigmatic weight, and Alex could instantly tell that he would most likely do well not to trifle with them. "You have been called here for a purpose, Alex," the figure continued.

Alex calculated in his mind that since he could swear that he had never met such an entity in his life before, there should have been no way to know him by name. But within the past few hours, Alex's known reality had already proven to be quite incomplete of a reference, which is why he decided not to brood over it. If it was indeed as it seemed, and he was in the presence of a celestial being, he wouldn't be surprised if they knew his whole life story. He decided to not say a word and just listen for now.

Chapter 2

The Hero of Echoes

“I am Luna, the threshold guardian of Echoes,” the figure introduced itself to Alex. “I have been awaiting your arrival here, from whence your destiny begins. I shall be your guide and your wisdom in this realm, for you have a duty to fulfill - one that only you are capable of.”

Destiny...? Duty...? Alex was confused by those words. The journey up until now had been quite exciting, having found himself in a totally different realm with new and unique experiences waiting at its every corner. But right now, things were starting to look iffy - the last thing he wanted was to be burdened with undisclosed responsibilities and unrealistic expectations in a realm he barely knew. He knew he would have a difficult time dodging them were he to find himself in such a situation - that is if he had any choice in the first place.

“Fret Not” Luna’s golden eyes were studying and most likely had deciphered what was going on in Alex’s mind. “It’s your own destiny. You cannot escape it, but fortunately, you don't need to. All you need is the courage to accept it."

"What is this destiny that you speak of?" Alex finally spoke, getting right into the detail.

"Our world, Echoes, is at peril, Alex, and you have a rare gift that can help us - the gift of being able to see the threads that weave reality and myth together, a gift you've yet to fully understand. It's my duty to be your aid and help you understand what you need to. Do you know what this place is, Alex?" Luna concluded for now with an inquiry.

"Echoes - you said, right? Unfortunately, no, considering I haven't yet received the official guidebook for this place," Alex responded. He realized immediately that his habit of resorting to jest in serious situations might land him with some severe consequences for once.

"Oh, but you have, Alex. Or would you prefer if I took on the form of a more conventional guidebook from your world?" Luna responded. Alex could almost make out a hint of a smile concealed within the celestial features of her face. "No, I think I prefer it this way," Alex quipped fast.

A moment of silence elapsed before a slight chuckle by Luna broke it. “You have a way with words, Alex,” she said.

“Thanks, I’ve been told that before.”

"Your journey must have been tiring, Alex. You should take a moment to relax," Luna said, leading him to a moss-covered rock bathed in the soft glow of moonlight. As is your destiny, we must continue forward, but there’s no harm in a breather once in a while, is there? Take this time to try to align yourself with the essence of Echoes. Breathe, and let its magic fill your spirit."

As they sat together in the tranquil clearing, Alex closed his eyes, inhaling the sweet fragrance of the surrounding flora. The cool breeze carried with it a sense of serenity, a brief respite from the impending journey. Luna's presence provided comfort, and the moonlit landscape seemed to cradle them in its ethereal embrace.

"Feel the connection between yourself and this mystical realm," Luna encouraged, her voice like a soothing echo. "Let the energy of Echoes rejuvenate your spirit before we tread deeper into the heart of the forest."

Taking a few moments to absorb the enchanting ambiance, Alex felt a newfound calm wash over him. Luna's wisdom and the magic of Echoes worked in harmony, offering a brief interlude in the moonlit clearing—a sanctuary before the challenges that lay ahead.

Refreshed and centered, Alex rose from the mossy rock, ready to continue their journey into the mysterious depths of Echoes. Luna, with a knowing smile, gestured for him to follow, the moonlight guiding their path through the whispering trees.

As they ventured deeper into the moonlit forest, the ethereal glow of Echoes guiding their way, Luna began to share more about their impending journey.

"We'll be heading for the long-forgotten Cavern of Shadows, where the source of the darkness was first detected by the Elders of this realm," Luna explained to Alex. "We must investigate what it is that challenges the very survival of our world, and yours. But first, we'll be going through the Valley of Whispers. Theron, the warrior, waits for us there to join us in our quest. I'm sure he'll be an invaluable asset to our cause."

A sense of purpose resonated in Luna's words, but Alex couldn't help but feel a mixture of curiosity and apprehension. "The Valley of Whispers," he mused. "That sounds like a place with its own tales to tell."

Luna nodded in agreement, her golden eyes reflecting the ancient wisdom she carried. "Indeed. The Valley is a place where echoes of forgotten whispers linger. It holds memories of ages past, and its mystical energy resonates with the very essence of Echoes."

As they continued their journey through the moonlit forest, the trees seemed to whisper secrets, their leaves rustling with untold stories. The air crackled with magic, and Alex found himself drawn into the mystique of the Valley of Whispers.

Curiosity got the better of him, and Alex couldn't resist asking, "Tell me more about the Elders. Who are they, and how do they sense the darkness that threatens Echoes?"

They are the guardians of ancient knowledge, keepers of the balance in Echoes," Luna began, her voice carrying the weight of ages. "Connected to the energies that flow through the very fabric of this realm, they sense disturbances that could jeopardize its existence."

Alex, fascinated, pressed for more details. "How do they sense these disturbances? Is it some kind of mystical intuition?"

Luna nodded, her silver hair catching the moonlight. "It's a deep connection, Alex. An intuition honed over centuries. They feel the ebb and flow of Echoes, attuned to the subtle shifts that ripple through the very essence of our world."

Having briefly explained the role of the Elders, she turned the conversation towards Alex. "And what of you, Alex? Before you found yourself here, what were the echoes of your world that resonated within you?"

Alex contemplated Luna's question, the memories of his life back in the mundane world intertwining with the enchantment of Echoes. He spoke of his love for storytelling, the passion that fueled his imagination, and the countless tales he had written and left unfinished.

Luna listened intently, her celestial features reflecting genuine interest. "Stories have a way of connecting worlds, Alex. Your journey may have started in your world, but now you're woven into the tapestry of Echoes. The threads of your stories intertwine with the very essence of this realm," she recognized the uniqueness of Alex's own story.

The moonlit forest continued to unfold around them as they delved deeper into the Valley of Whispers, its mystical aura enveloping Alex and Luna. The journey had become more than just a quest; it was a convergence of destinies, a dance between the known and the unknown. As they continued walking for the next few hours, the moonlight casting enchanting shadows, Alex couldn't help but wonder about the challenges that awaited him in the Valley of Whispers and beyond.

Their journey was abruptly halted by a luminous barrier, a sudden twist that jolted the forest's serene ambiance. Shimmering across their path, the barrier added an air of mystery and intrigue, capturing the moonlight in a dance of ethereal hues.

"We must have reached the entrance to the Valley. To pass, a truth must be revealed," Luna spoke, her voice carrying the weight of ancient secrets. "A story from your heart," she continued, "One that hasn't been told and is known only by you."

Alex's mind raced, urgency coursing through his veins. He thought of his unfinished manuscripts, the parchment of untold stories yearning for completion. And yet, here he could rely only on his own story - one that was embarrassing, frustrating, and sometimes hilarious.

In the hush of the moonlit clearing, Alex took a deep breath and summoned the courage to share a tale he had guarded like a closely kept secret – a cringe-worthy incident that, once laid bare, had no coming back from.

With an almost imperceptible sigh, he began, "Alright, fine. Brace yourself for a tale that will forever mark me as the uncrowned king of eccentricity." The scene unfolded to a peculiar open-mic night at a dimly lit café, a setting he had tried so hard to erase from memory.

"Picture this," he continued with a half-smirk, "me, decked out in an ensemble that defies both fashion and reason. The music, an avant-garde symphony of classical meets electronic chaos. And there I am, on that tiny stage, embracing interpretive dance as my chosen form of expression."

The reluctant admission hung in the air as he recounted the contortions of limbs that had defied both gravity and the laws of conventional dance. "The café was my canvas, and I was painting a masterpiece of bewildering moves. I'm talking interpretive dance that left even the most open-minded patrons questioning the very fabric of reality."

The moonlit clearing seemed to absorb the absurdity, and Luna's gaze held a mix of amusement and genuine surprise. "Yes, Luna, you heard it right. I, the mighty Alex, once subjected unsuspecting souls to a spectacle that bordered on the surreal."

“That’s definitely a memory worth preserving, Alex,” Luna said as she tried her best to keep her amusement from erupting. “And now, for better or worse, it’s been etched permanently into my memory as well!” A wide grin almost broke out on Luna’s face despite her best efforts to conceal it, prompting a sharp look from Alex.

“Well, I’m glad you didn’t have to share your embarrassing memories. And don’t try telling me you have none,” he said.

Luna responded with a smile of childish mischief before the two once again set out on their journey. As Alex and Luna found themselves on the threshold of the Valley of Whispers, the transition was as abrupt as a shift in dimensions, and the atmosphere underwent a dramatic transformation.

The enchanted and mystical forest landscape, with its towering trees and moonlit foliage, now gave way to the Valley of Whispers — a vast expanse bathed in a diffused, ethereal glow. The moon's radiance seemed to linger, casting an otherworldly pallor over the landscape. The trees, once densely packed, now stood with more intentional spacing, their gnarled branches reaching toward the heavens like ancient sentinels.

The air, once thick with the scent of pine and earth, carried a different fragrance—an intoxicating blend of mystic herbs and the faint, elusive aroma of long-forgotten tales. The ground beneath their feet felt softer, a carpet of velvety moss that seemed to absorb the whispers of centuries gone by.

As the moon dipped low and the break of daylight was right on the verge, a gentle glow blanketed the Valley of Whispers. Alex found himself mesmerized by what he was seeing, now that they could start seeing much better. The trees, the birds, the grass, everything seemed like they were plucked straight out of a painting.

“Look! A river,” Luna exclaimed. "How about a quick wash to shake off the enchantment of the Whispering Woods? The river looks inviting, doesn't it?"

Alex nodded in agreement, and they both made their way to the riverbank. The cool water beckoned, and Alex splashed his face while Luna gracefully dipped her hands, letting the essence of Echoes cleanse their spirits.

Deciding to linger a bit by the river, Luna smiled and said, "Let's make a moment of it. Feel the magic of Echoes in the water. It has a way of rejuvenating the spirit."

As they took in the serenity of the river, Luna decided to set up a small fire near the riverbank. Gathering twigs and leaves, she expertly kindled a flame that flickered in tune with the enchantment of the valley. Seeing Luna's skillful fire-making, Alex couldn't help but admire her resourcefulness. "You're quite adept with the elemental arts, Luna."

With a modest grin, she replied, "It's a skill learned over time. Fire has its own way of connecting with the energies around us."

As the flames crackled and danced, Luna's eyes flickered with a playful glint. "Now, how about some breakfast? Maybe a catch from this lovely river?" she suggested, gesturing towards the fish that darted beneath the surface.

"As you wish, my lady," Alex gestured a courteous tip and got to work. He fashioned a basic fishing rod from nearby branches and started casting into the clear waters.

Ever since he was a child, his father had been taking him fishing every Sunday. Skills such as these – he had already developed by the time he was 10. A fleeting sense of nostalgia washed over him as he wondered how his father had been doing. It had been quite a few years now since the last time they went fishing together. The anticipation of a fresh catch, however, added a touch of excitement to the tranquil morning as Alex shifted his mind's attention back to the present moment.

The aroma of cooking fish slowly began to mingle with the morning air as Alex and Luna sat by the crackling fire, the river softly murmuring in the background. Luna gazed into the flames, her eyes reflecting the flickering dance of the firelight.

Alex, tending to the fish on the makeshift grill, couldn't help but comment on the simplicity of the meal. "There's something about the basics, isn't there? A good catch, a warm fire, it feels... grounding."

Luna smiled in agreement. "Indeed, Alex. In the heart of simplicity, we often find the most profound connections with the world around us."

As he turned the fish to cook them on the other side, a look of curiosity formed on Alex's face. "Speaking of connections, tell me more about Echoes. These tales you've been sharing, they're like whispers from another world."

"Echoes is a realm where reality and myth intertwine. It's a place where the threads of stories are woven into the very fabric of existence. The ancient energies here connect with the essence of every tale, creating a tapestry that spans beyond time," her eyes almost sparkled as she spoke. It was clearly visible how much she loved and cared for her realm.

Alex probed further. "And what about you, Luna? What's your role in all of this? Besides being an excellent guide and fire conjurer."

Luna chuckled, the warmth of the fire reflecting in her eyes. "I am the threshold guardian, a keeper of wisdom in Echoes. My duty is to aid those who possess the rare gift of perceiving the threads that weave reality and myth together. In you, Alex, I sense a unique connection to the stories that echo through time."

Alex didn't know quite how to feel, but by now, he had already formed his resolve. He didn't quite know yet what his connection with this place was, but if this was his destiny, he would shoulder it. Amidst the crackling of the fire, the river's gentle murmurs, and the aroma of the cooking fish, their conversation flowed like a tranquil stream of understanding—a dialogue that wove the present with the ancient tales of Echoes.

Suddenly, the air changed, and a low growl echoed through the valley. A huge ogre appeared from nowhere, drawn by the scent of cooking fish. Luna's eyes widened as the creature lumbered towards them.

Panicking, Alex turned to Luna, "Can you fight, Luna?"

She chuckled, "Oh, Alex, my skills are in guidance and wisdom, not brawn. We might need more than magical whispers this time."

The two immediately start running, being chased by the ogre. Its laughter echoed through the valley as it rampaged through the trees, seemingly enjoying the chase quite a bit. The chase weaved through the river and the trees, the two desperately trying to hold on to their lives when suddenly a booming voice halted the ogre right in its tracks, "Hold, foul creature!"

Chapter 3

Encounter with an Assassin

As an imposing armor-clad figure stood off with the brutish ogre with a huge, worn-looking but thoroughly maintained sword, Luna turned to Alex with urgency in her voice. "That's Theron, Alex," she informed, her voice tinged with relief. "He's an ancient warrior, a guardian of Echoes. We're fortunate to have him by our side."

Watching the battle unfold, Alex felt a mixture of awe and apprehension. "He's... formidable," he remarked quietly, his gaze fixed on Theron's battle-scarred armor as he skillfully parried the ogre's strikes.

With each clash of steel against club, Theron's experience and skill became evident. He moved with a fluidity that belied his heavy armor, each strike calculated and precise. The ogre, a hulking mass of muscle and fury, roared with each blow, but Theron remained unfazed, his determination unwavering.

Finally, with a decisive blow, Theron incapacitated the ogre, sending it crashing to the ground with a resounding thud. As the echoes of the battle faded, he turned to face Alex and Luna, his expression unreadable beneath his battle-worn helm.

As Luna turned to Theron, curiosity shining in her eyes, she couldn't help but wonder. "How did you know we were in danger, Theron? Your timely arrival saved us."

Theron's gaze softened slightly, a hint of amusement glinting in his eyes. "The commotion of the ogre was enough to catch my attention," he explained simply, his voice carrying the weight of his centuries of experience. "In a place like this, one learns to be attuned to the signs of danger."

Luna nodded thoughtfully, a sense of gratitude coloring her expression. "Your vigilance is appreciated, Theron. Your presence brings us a sense of security in these uncertain times."

As they exchanged silent acknowledgments, Alex couldn't help but marvel at the unspoken bond between Luna and Theron—a connection forged through countless trials and shared experiences. In that moment, he realized the depth of the challenges they faced and the importance of their alliance in navigating the treacherous path ahead.

Stepping forward, Luna introduced Alex to Theron, emphasizing his unique connection to the stories of Echoes. Theron's skepticism was evident as he turned his gaze to Alex, his voice low and rumbling. "A human in the Valley of Whispers," he mused. "What brings you here, Alex? What business do you have in our realm?"

Feeling the weight of Theron's scrutiny, Alex straightened his posture, his thoughts swirling with confusion and determination. "I'll be honest, Theron," he began, his voice steady despite the uncertainty. "I'm just as puzzled as you are. Suddenly being thrust into this realm and told of some 'destiny'—it's all a bit overwhelming... But what I do know is that there's a deep connection between this realm and mine, and as long as danger looms over Echoes, I can't turn a blind eye. So, I'm here to do what needs to be done."

Theron's gaze lingered, his expression inscrutable. After a moment of silence, he nodded, a gesture of reluctant acceptance. "Very well, Alex," he conceded. "I will aid you in your journey but know this — the road ahead is fraught with peril. The challenges you face will test you like never before. I am curious to see how you will fare."

With Theron's reluctant agreement, the tension between them eased slightly, though an unspoken understanding hung in the air—a sense that their alliance was forged on uncertain ground.

"Hey, since we're not in immediate danger anymore, maybe we should go back to the river and see if those fishes we were frying are still edible. All that running made me even hungrier!" Alex couldn't help but further lighten the mood with his suggestion.

Theron let out a resigned sigh at Alex's suggestion but nodded in agreement nonetheless. With a subtle gesture, he retrieved a small, intricately embroidered pouch from his belt. With a flick of his wrist, he opened it to pour out an array of food items and drinks one after the other, each more tantalizing than the last.

Alex's eyes widened in amazement as he took in the sight. There were golden pastries filled with savory meats, succulent fruits bursting with juice, and bottles of sparkling beverages that seemed to shimmer in the sunlight. It was a feast fit for kings, conjured seemingly out of thin air.

"How... where did you get all this?" Alex asked, his excitement barely contained.

Theron offered him a small, knowing smile. "It's a little something I picked up along the way," he replied cryptically, his eyes twinkling with amusement.

Turning to Luna, Alex couldn't help but ask, "Did you have one of those too?"

Luna chuckled softly, her eyes alight with affection. "Yes, I did," she admitted. "I just felt like watching you catch those fishes would be entertaining - and I was right!"

"Ugh, "Alex seemed done with her. With a sigh of surrender, he let it go. Their journey had only just started, and for some reason, Alex couldn't imagine that it would end soon enough. He supposed he would have to put up with much more than this over the course of it.

With their hunger sated and their spirits replenished, they set off once more, on their quest to make it past the Valley of Whispers. As they continued their journey, the day stretched on, and Alex couldn't shake the feeling of being watched. Every now and then, he caught snippets of ethereal whispers dancing on the breeze, their voices echoing through the trees like distant echoes of forgotten memories.

Curiosity gnawed at him, and he turned to Luna with a furrowed brow. "What are those whispers, Luna? They're... unsettling."

Luna's gaze softened, her eyes scanning the shadowy depths of the valley. "The whispers are the voices of the past, Alex," she explained gently. "They are the echoes of long-forgotten tales and ancient secrets that linger in the air, haunting this valley for eternity."

As they walked, conversation flowed more casually between them, Theron occasionally interjecting with dry humor and unexpected anecdotes from his years of experience. Suddenly, without warning, the ground beneath their feet began to tremble, and the air crackled with an otherworldly energy. Luna's eyes widened in alarm, and she exchanged a tense glance with Theron."What's happening?" Alex exclaimed, his heart pounding with unease.

Before anyone could respond, the very fabric of reality seemed to warp and shift around them, and with a deafening roar, a portal ripped open in front of them, bathing them in blinding light. As they stumbled backward, a figure emerged from the portal, its form shrouded in darkness. With a chilling certainty, Luna whispered, "It seems we're not alone in the Valley of Whispers."

As the figure emerged from the portal, its presence cast a shadow over the group, sending shivers down their spines. Its features were obscured by darkness, but its aura exuded an ominous energy that chilled them to the bone.

Theron instinctively stepped forward, his hand tightening around the hilt of his sword. "Who are you?" he demanded, his voice commanding despite the unease that gnawed at him.

The figure remained silent, its gaze fixed on Luna with an intensity that sent a chill down Alex's spine. Luna, though visibly shaken, met its gaze with unwavering resolve.

"Be careful, Theron. Those obscure features and those glowing red eyes... There's no doubt. Our attacker is a member of Skavari, a race of trained assassins from the Shadow realm," Luna whispered urgently, her voice barely above a breath.

Alex's heart pounded in his chest as he processed Luna's words. "If that's the case, it means someone wants at least one or, possibly, all of us dead," he realized aloud, his voice tinged with apprehension.

Theron's grip tightened on his sword, his gaze never leaving the figure before them. "We cannot let our guard down," he warned, his tone grave. "Whatever their intentions, we must be prepared to defend ourselves."

The Skavari let out a low, guttural growl that sent a ripple of fear through the group. With a sudden burst of movement, it lunged forward, its form shifting and contorting in the dim light.

Theron reacted with lightning speed, his sword slicing through the air with precision. But to his surprise, the figure seemed to dissipate into shadows, reforming behind him with unsettling fluidity. As Theron's sword struggled to keep up with the assassin's, Alex's mind raced with fear and uncertainty. With each passing moment, the situation seemed to grow more dire, and he realized that they were facing an adversary unlike any they had encountered before.

A fierce duel between Theron and the Skavari continued, their blades clashing with a ferocity that echoed through the valley. But despite Theron's formidable skill, it was getting clearer by the second that it wasn't enough to avert the imminent crisis. Luna watched with growing desperation, her mind racing as she searched for a way to turn the tide of battle. Theron fought with unmatched determination, but he needed some backup - fast.

As the confrontation reached a critical juncture, Alex began hearing a faint whisper that seemed to call out to him. He reluctantly turned his attention from the clash towards the whisper, trying to figure out the source of it when he realized - it was the whispers of the valley. They were trying to tell him something, and in order to understand what it was, Alex focused his mind.

In the next few moments, Alex felt a sort of connection with Echoes like he never had. He could sense the cosmic energies surge through him. Something inside him told him exactly what to do with that energy. He put together his hands, focused his mind, and began casting a spell of his own creation.

The bright flash of blue light emerging from her side took Luna by surprise as she turned to see something that she really didn't expect - a beam of blue light shot out of Alex's palms and launched itself right at the Skavarian. Before anyone in the fray could react, the burst of ethereal energy engulfed its target, dispersing it in a blinding flash of light.

The valley fell silent as the echoes of battle faded, leaving behind only the soft rustle of leaves in the breeze. Theron staggered back, his breath ragged as he surveyed the scene before him. Alex glanced at Theron, a sense of gratitude and respect passing between them.

“You saved my life, Alex. Thank you,” said Theron.

“Oh, let’s not make a big deal of it now. You scratch my back, I scratch yours. I reckon we might need to continue with that working arrangement for a while now,” Alex responded.

“I didn’t know you could use magic, Alex. When did you learn that?” asked Luna curiously.

“I didn't know I could either. I think the whispers of the valley taught me right now,” he explained.

“That’s interesting…” Luna seemed to be deep in thought as she replied. She had never witnessed anything such as this before and wondered if this was a part of Alex’s latent power or if he had been granted this ability because of his destined role.

As the group caught their breath after the intense confrontation, they gathered to discuss the events that had transpired. Theron's brow furrowed in deep concentration as he tried to make sense of their attacker's motives.

"Why would a trained assassin from another realm come after us?" Alex wondered aloud, his voice tinged with confusion. "What could they possibly want with us?"

Luna shook her head, her expression troubled. "Without more information, it's difficult to say," she admitted. "But one thing's for certain — we can't afford to let our guard down."

Theron nodded in agreement, his gaze scanning the surrounding shadows for any sign of further danger. "Nightfall is imminent," he observed, his voice grim. "It might be risky to continue traveling, especially since we might get attacked again. We should seek shelter somewhere nearby until dawn."

Luna nodded in agreement, relief washing over her at the prospect of finding shelter for the night. "There's a village nestled by the lake not far from here," she suggested. "It should provide us with a safe haven until morning."

Theron's eyes brightened at the mention of the village. "Yes, that sounds like our best option," he agreed. "We can rest there and regroup before heading to the mountains at first light."

With their course of action decided, the group set off toward the village, the glow of distant lights guiding their way through the gathering dusk. As they continued their journey through the Valley of Whispers, Alex couldn't shake the feeling of power coursing through him. With each step forward, he knew that he had unlocked a new chapter in his journey—one filled with untold challenges and boundless potential. And with Theron and Luna by his side, he was ready to face whatever lay ahead.

"There! There's the village of Turtle-blue," exclaimed Luna, her voice carrying a note of relief as a distant cluster of buildings drew nearer.

The sun dipped low on the horizon, casting a warm golden glow over the landscape. The village emerged like a picturesque scene from a storybook, its thatched cottages and cobblestone streets bathed in the soft light of dusk. Once at the gateway, they were halted by guards who eyed them with cautious interest, their armor glinting in the fading sunlight.

Alex noticed the intricate carvings on the gateposts, depicting scenes from local folklore while Luna attended to the guards. "We're travelers seeking shelter for the night," she explained, her tone friendly yet cautious. Satisfied with their answer, the guards let them pass, and they wandered into the heart of the village.

Once inside, the village revealed itself to be a bustling hub of activity. Colorful market stalls lined the streets, offering an array of goods ranging from freshly picked fruits to handcrafted wares. The air was alive with the sound of vendors hawking their wares and the laughter of children playing in the nearby square.

Amidst the hustle and bustle, Alex couldn't help but notice the unique architecture of the buildings. Each cottage seemed to have its

own story to tell, with ivy-clad walls and quaint window boxes overflowing with vibrant flowers.

As they made their way through the village, they passed by a lively tavern, its door propped open invitingly with the words hanging above, “The Turtle’s Tavern”. The tantalizing aroma of sizzling food wafted out, tempting their senses and prompting their stomachs to rumble in anticipation. Deciding to grab a bite to eat before finding lodging, they settled inside.

The atmosphere was as welcoming as it could get, with merry men drinking after a long, hard day of work and lively young women serving the tables. And yet, Alex couldn't shake the feeling of being watched. He caught glimpses of curious faces peering out from behind curtains and doorways, their eyes following their every move with a mixture of curiosity and suspicion. It couldn't be helped though - their group did stand out quite a bit amidst the usuals and the locals. Despite the undercurrent of tension, there was an undeniable charm to the village of Turtle-blue.

As they enjoyed their meal, the three engaging each other in each other's stories and experiences, Alex's curiosity got the better of him.

"Why is this place called Turtle-blue?" he asked, glancing at Luna.

"Legend has it that there was once a wise blue turtle that lived in the lake here," she explained. "It was said to possess great wisdom and was revered by the villagers. But unfortunately, that was hundreds of years ago. No one knows what happened to the turtle."

"That's... a bit sad," Alex exclaimed.

After dinner, Luna and Theron retired to their own rooms while Alex found himself unable to shake off a sense of restlessness. The warmth and camaraderie of the tavern had only served to amplify his inner turmoil. With a quiet determination, he slipped out into the cool night air, the cobblestone streets bathing in the soft silver light of the moon.

As he walked, the gentle rustle of leaves and the distant murmur of the village faded into the background. Alex's steps led him towards the lake, drawn by an inexplicable pull towards its tranquil waters. The moon cast a luminous path across the surface, guiding his way as he ventured deeper into the night.

Arriving at the water's edge, Alex found a secluded spot to sit and contemplate. The night was still, broken only by the gentle lapping of the lake against the shore. He gazed out across the dark expanse, the reflection of the moon shimmering on the calm surface.

Lost in thought, Alex found himself pondering the events of the day—the unexpected attack, the mysteries of Echoes, and his own burgeoning powers. With each passing moment, the weight of his newfound responsibilities seemed to grow heavier, pressing down on him like an invisible burden.

Suddenly, without warning, a dense white mist began to form around him, swirling and twirling as if guided by some unseen force. The air grew thick with moisture, and Alex found himself enveloped in an eerie silence, the only sound the steady rhythm of his own heartbeat echoing in the stillness of the night.

Chapter 4

The Blue Turtle

As the mist slowly dissipated, Alex blinked in astonishment, his eyes widening in disbelief at the sight before him. There, towering over him, was a gigantic bluish-hued turtle, bathed in an ethereal glow. It was a creature unlike any he had ever seen before, its majestic form at least three times his size.

At first, shock held Alex in its grip, his mind struggling to comprehend the surreal sight. Then, a surge of excitement and curiosity washed over him, driving away his initial apprehension. With trembling hands, he reached out tentatively, almost afraid to confirm that the creature was real. "Are you... are you the legendary Blue Turtle?" Alex stammered, his voice tinged with awe and wonder.

The turtle regarded him with ancient eyes, its gaze wise and penetrating. "I've been known by that name once upon a time, although there's hardly anyone to call me that anymore," it replied, its voice resonating with a deep sense of wisdom. "I am the guardian of these waters, keeper of the secrets that lie within."

As Alex's heart pounded with anticipation, he dared to venture further. "You called me here for a reason, didn't you?" he ventured, his voice filled with a mixture of curiosity and trepidation.

The Blue Turtle nodded solemnly. "Indeed, young traveler," it confirmed, its tone grave. "For I have sensed a disturbance in the inner flow of Echoes—a disruption that threatens to unravel the very fabric of existence."

Alex furrowed his brow in confusion. "What do you mean by the 'inner flow'? And more importantly, what exactly is Echoes? I feel like I need to know more about that," he asked, his curiosity piqued.

The Blue Turtle inclined its massive head, as if preparing to impart ancient wisdom. "Echoes is more than just a realm, Alex," it explained patiently. "It is a tapestry of interconnected energies, woven together by the threads of time and space in the form of what we call the Origin Tree. Every event, every action, sends ripples through this fabric, shaping the course of destiny itself and keeping the universe in perfect harmony as a whole. If the disruption isn't taken care of, I'm afraid it might not be a stretch to assume that the whole universe is in grave threat."

Alex listened intently, hanging on the Blue Turtle's every word. "But what does this have to do with me? I'm just a writer from another realm" he pressed, his mind racing with questions.

The Blue Turtle fixed him with a solemn gaze. "You are the bridge between worlds, Alex," it revealed, its voice carrying the weight of centuries. "Your presence here is no accident. You possess a rare gift—the ability to perceive the subtle currents that flow between Echoes and your own world."

Alex felt a sense of realization wash over him. "That would explain how I've always felt like I had too vivid of an imagination," he surmised.

As Alex absorbed the enormity of the revelation, the Blue Turtle continued to unravel the mysteries of Echoes, explaining its connection to his own home world and the importance of maintaining balance between the realms.

"And it is within the depths of the Cavern of Shadows that the disturbance emerges from," the Blue Turtle revealed, its voice carrying a solemn weight. "A darkness stirs, threatening to disrupt the delicate equilibrium that sustains our realms."

Alex still had a few questions regarding Echoes and the cultures within in, but he felt like all those could wait. He couldn't help but wonder about the Blue Turtle's prolonged absence. "Why have you remained hidden for centuries?" Alex asked, his voice tinged with curiosity.

The Blue Turtle's ancient eyes seemed to hold a hint of sorrow. "I have been magically sealed within the depths of this lake by a powerful sorceress," it explained, its voice tinged with regret. "Since then, I have been unable to communicate with anyone beyond these waters. It is only through your unique gift of perception that I am able to reach out and impart my knowledge."

Alex's heart swelled with empathy for the creature before him. He had been chosen as the bridge between worlds, tasked with unraveling the mysteries of Echoes and restoring balance to the realms. But at the same time, he also wanted to do good for the inhabitants of Echoes that he would come across in his journey.

"Is there anything I can do to free you from your imprisonment?" he asked.

The Blue Turtle regarded him with a solemn expression, its ancient eyes reflecting a depth of wisdom that transcended time itself. "There is a magical item that holds the key to my release," it revealed, its voice carrying a faint tremor of hope. "The Crystal of Unsealing, hidden within the depths of the Mountain of Echo. But there's really no need to trouble yourself with that, Alex. You have far more important duties to perform here."

Alex's mind raced with determination as he absorbed the significance of the task ahead. "The Mountain of Echo," he repeated, his voice tinged with determination. "That's where we're headed next."

The Blue Turtle nodded gravely, its majestic form radiating a sense of quiet resolve. "Indeed, the path to the Mountain of Echo lies along the way to the Caverns of Shadows," it confirmed. "But tread carefully, young traveler, for the mountains are unforgiving, and the dangers that await are beyond reckoning, especially if you're planning to scale it for the Crystal," its voice echoed as the white mist enveloped Alex once again, bringing him back to where he had been.

As the morning sun of the next day cast its golden rays over the village of Turtle-blue,

Alex awoke from his restless slumber, the memory of his encounter with the Blue Turtle still fresh in his mind. Pushing aside the lingering tendrils of sleep, he rose from his bed and made his way downstairs to join Luna and Theron for breakfast.

As they gathered around the table, the trio exchanged quiet greetings, their expressions a mix of anticipation and determination. Luna wasted no time in laying out their plan for the day, her voice crisp and decisive.

"We'll need to make our way to the foothills of Mount Echo to meet with Eirys the healer," she began, her gaze sweeping over the map spread out before them. "From there, we'll assess our next steps in crossing the mountains."

Alex hesitated for a moment, his thoughts still consumed by his conversation with the Blue Turtle. "Actually, I had a different idea," he interjected, his voice tentative yet resolute.

Luna arched an eyebrow inquisitively, her curiosity piqued. "Oh? And what might that be?" she asked, her tone tinged with a hint of skepticism.

"I met the Blue Turtle last night," Alex confessed, his voice filled with quiet determination as he explained the whole thing to her. "It told me about the Crystal of Unsealing, and how it's the key to freeing it from its imprisonment."

Luna's eyes widened in surprise, her expression a mix of awe and concern. "The Crystal of Unsealing?" she echoed, her voice barely above a whisper. "But Alex, finding it will be an incredibly difficult task. It could take us weeks, even months."

Alex nodded, undeterred by the daunting prospect. "I know it won't be easy," he admitted, his gaze steady. "But I want to help the Blue Turtle. It's been trapped for centuries, and it's about time someone did something about it."

Theron, who had been listening quietly, cleared his throat, his deep voice cutting through the conversation like a thunderclap. "While I understand your noble intentions, Alex, we mustn't lose sight of our primary objective," he reminded them, his tone firm yet measured.

Luna nodded in agreement, her expression thoughtful. "Theron's right. Our main goal is to reach the Caverns of Shadows and uncover the source of the disturbance," she acknowledged. "But perhaps we can find a way to help the Blue Turtle on our return journey through the mountains. Moreover, I'm really jealous you got to meet the legendary Blue Turtle, Alex. I'm sure I'll have a lot to learn from such an ancient and wise being."

Alex's lips curled into a determined smile, his resolve unwavering. "Agreed," he declared, his voice tinged with determination. "But for now, let's focus on reaching Eirys and assessing the situation at hand."

They finished their breakfast and prepared to set out once more, their shared purpose driving them forward into the unknown. The journey through the rugged terrain of the foothills proved to be arduous yet exhilarating, each step bringing them closer to their destination. Luna led the way with confidence, her knowledge of the trails guiding them through winding paths and rocky outcrops.

As they approached Eirys' humble hut, nestled amidst the towering peaks, the warm aroma of freshly cooked food wafted through the crisp mountain air, tantalizing their senses and stirring their appetites. Luna rapped on the door, the sound echoing through the quiet solitude of the mountains.

Moments later, the door swung open to reveal Eirys, a kind smile lighting up her weathered face. "Come in," she greeted them warmly, her voice as gentle as the mountain breeze. "Lunch is ready."

The interior of the hut was cozy and inviting, the crackling fire from the hearth casting dancing shadows across the walls. Eirys motioned for them to take a seat at the rough-hewn table, where steaming bowls of hearty stew awaited them. As they ate, conversation flowed freely, the group discussing their journey thus far and the challenges that lay ahead.

"The Cavern of Whispers has always been a place shrouded in mystery," Luna explained, her voice tinged with a hint of solemnity. "Legend has it that it was once home to an ancient civilization, but now it's said to be haunted by restless spirits and dark creatures."

Theron nodded in agreement, his expression grave. "It's the kind of place you usually want to stay away from," he added, his voice low and foreboding.

After lunch, as the sun dipped below the horizon and darkness descended upon the foothills, Eirys suggested that they set out next morning instead. "The trails become treacherous after dark," she warned them, her tone somber. "It's best to wait until dawn to continue your journey."

Theron agreed with her, emphasizing that they couldn't yet risk to encounter the monsters that lurk in the night. Eirys offered them all a change of clothes to make themselves comfortable. Luna suggested they take the party outside for a while before sleeping the night off and set up a campfire in the yard.

"We need to go to sleep early, but it won't hurt us to get to know each other a bit more," she said. As they sat around the fire outside, the atmosphere grew relaxed and jovial, the warmth of the flames chasing away the chill of the mountain air. Eirys brought out drinks, and soon they found themselves laughing and sharing stories late into the night.

The conversation meandered from tales of adventure to hopes and dreams for the future, each of them opening up in their own ways. Amidst the laughter and banter, bonds were forged that would carry them through the trials yet to come, uniting them in their quest.

"So, Alex," Luna began with a playful glint in her eyes, "tell us more about your encounter with the Blue Turtle. Did it give you any cryptic prophecies or ancient wisdom?"

Alex chuckled, taking a sip of the offered drink. "Well, it did reveal that I'm the chosen one destined to save Echoes from certain doom," he replied with a mock-serious expression, earning a round of laughter from the group.

Theron raised an eyebrow, a hint of amusement dancing in his eyes. "Ah, the chosen one," he mused. "I suppose that makes you our fearless leader, then?"

Alex grinned, shaking his head. "Hardly," he admitted with a self-deprecating laugh. "But I do feel a sense of duty to help however I can."

Eirys, her gentle voice tinged with curiosity, leaned forward. "And what about you, Luna? Have you ever encountered the Blue Turtle before?"

A look of wishfulness washed over her face as she replied, “No, I haven’t. But I would certainly love to if I had the chance.”

Theron, ever the stoic warrior, observed the conversation with a quiet intensity. "Legends and prophecies aside," he interjected, "we must remain vigilant. The dangers we face are real, and we cannot afford to underestimate them."

Alex nodded in agreement, his expression turning serious. "You're right, Theron," he conceded. "But for now, let's enjoy this moment of respite. Who knows what tomorrow may bring?"

With that, they raised their glasses in a silent toast, celebrating their last drinks for the night before retiring back into the hut.

Chapter 5

Visions of the Past

As the dark grey clouds partially veiled the reddish sky of a dying realm, the dry and barren landscape below lay reminiscent of a once-flourishing ecosystem that seemed to be growing more and more diseased. The ground cracked and parched, whispering tales of a forgotten vitality.

"Alteoth, you will hereby be tried for your treason against your cause as a fellow God-Designer of the realm of Echoes and failing to guide your vassal to her destiny. You knew the consequences of your actions when you decided to conceive a child with her," said Ulther, the Chief of the Gods-Designers.

"Elana may have been a sacrificial pawn for you, but for me, she was the love of my life! All I wanted for her was a life worth living, but you wouldn't even let her have that!" retorted Alteoth angrily.

"She was the perfect vassal for the Origin Tree, Alteoth, and you knew that as well. But you couldn't even put aside your own feelings for the sake of your realm and so many others,"

Ulther said once again as the other God-Designers stood by silently, nodding in approval.

"If the realm needs the sacrifice of the life of my beloved to save itself, they can all go to hell – because Elana is dead," announced Alteoth loudly, hoping that it would satiate them to some extent.

"And you are responsible for that, Alteoth. You were the cause of her death," Ulther said calmly before continuing, "But don't worry. It's not yet the end of the world just yet. The blood of her lives on in your child, and now, she will have to carry on the responsibilities of her mother."

"No...! You can't do that," Alteoth screamed in rage and desperation. His mind raced at the thought of his daughter being taken away from him. Elara was the only one that he had left. Her red hair and beautiful eyes never failed to remind him of Elana, the mortal he had fallen in love with. The five-year-old was a spitting image of her mother, and he was determined to keep her away, safe from his fellow God-Designers. But now, he realized that he had failed to do so, because they had already come to know of her existence.

What Alteoth hadn't prepared for, however, was the horror that he was going to face. As a sentinel brought in his only child in chains in front of him by the orders of Ulther, Alteoth's emotions knew no bounds. His eyes broadened in shock and his body shook from head to toe.

"Papa –"Elara cried out as the sentinel dragged her and stood her right in front of Ulther and the others.

"Elara!" shouted Alteoth, his voice trembling in fear, rage, and desperation. He shifted his gaze next to Ulther and screamed, "Let her go! You have no right over her!"

"I hereby sentence," Ulther was in no mood to entertain as he began laying out his decision, "Alteoth to eternal ethereal imprisonment and Elara, the daughter of Alteoth and Elana, to assume the responsibilities of her mother – of becoming the vassal for the Origin Tree to bring all the realms together and connect the fabrics of reality to Echoes."

Ulther proceeded to chant a spell and Alteoth could only watch helplessly as a bright light enveloped Elara and slowly transformed her being into a transcendental tree with branches of energies originating from other realms connecting to the ground, gradually restoring the vitality of the land that had stood barren until now.

"NOOOO....!"

Alteoth's screams faded into the distant and barren landscape as suddenly, Alex woke up from his unusually vivid dream.

--

"Huh-!? What was that? A dream? The Origin Tree - was it real?" Alex muttered, his voice still laden with the echoes of his nightmare. He got up from his bed and looked out the window of the hut. It seemed daybreak was still a while away.

The other three were still fast asleep as Alex silently opened the door and walked outside, his mind going crazy with questions that he had no answers to yet. The air outside was cool, the darkness of the night enveloping him like a familiar cloak. He walked a few paces away from the hut, his thoughts swirling with uncertainty and confusion. As he gazed up at the starlit sky, a faint glimmer of determination flickered within him.

He took a deep breath and closed his eyes, focusing on the magic that lay dormant within him. With his arms extended forward from his body, he attempted to summon the same power he had wielded during their previous encounter. But to his dismay, nothing happened. Frustration gnawed at him as he tried again and again, each attempt met with failure.

Just as he was about to give up, a soft voice broke through the silence behind him. "Trying to practice your magic?" Luna's voice was laced with concern as she approached him.

"Yes," Alex confessed, his voice tinged with frustration. "But it's not working. And I don't understand why."

Luna placed a comforting hand on his shoulder. "Magic is not always about force, Alex," she said gently. "Sometimes, it's about letting go and allowing the energy to flow through you. Try to imagine the form of the magic, something that comes to you naturally."

Alex nodded, taking her words to heart. Closing his eyes once more, he delved deep into his thoughts, searching for something that felt right. Images flashed through his mind - the rush of the river, the crackling flames of the campfire, the gentle breeze against his skin.

With a newfound sense of focus, Alex tried again, this time envisioning the swirling currents of the river. Slowly, tentatively, he began to weave the magic, his hands moving in fluid motions as he conjured a shimmering orb of water. It hovered in the air before him, casting a soft glow in the darkness.

A smile tugged at the corners of Luna's lips as she watched him. "See? You just needed to find your own way," she said encouragingly.

Flushed with excitement, Alex continued to experiment, trying out different forms of magic. He conjured flames that danced in the night, summoned gusts of wind that rustled the leaves, and even attempted to shape the earth beneath his feet. Each attempt brought him closer to understanding his own abilities, his confidence growing with each success.

But despite his progress, there was still a lingering sense of unease in his heart. Turning to Luna, he voiced the question that had been weighing heavily on his mind. "Luna, what do you know about the Origin Tree?" he asked, his voice hushed with reverence.

Luna's expression grew solemn as she considered his question. "The Origin Tree has been here since time immemorial," she began, her voice carrying a note of reverence. "It is said to be the source of all magic in Echoes, holding the fabrics of the different realities together to prevent the realms from succumbing to darkness."

Alex listened intently, absorbing every word. "But why is it so important?" he pressed, his curiosity piqued.

"Because without the Origin Tree, the balance of the realms would be thrown into chaos," Luna explained. "It acts as a barrier, a guardian against the forces of darkness that seek to consume us. As long as the tree stands, Echoes will remain safe."

As the weight of Luna's words settled over him, Alex couldn't help but feel a sense of mixed feelings. The Origin Tree was not just a symbol of power – it was a beacon of hope in a world plagued by uncertainty. But if what he had seen was true, he couldn't help but feel for Elara and Alteoth.

“Is something wrong?” Luna asked, noticing his tensed expression.

“No, no... It's nothing,” Alex replied. He wasn't sure if he should discuss this, but for now, he chose to stay quiet about it until he knew something for certain.

“Did you lose your sleep as well?” he asked Luna.

“I sleep light. I saw you go out of the door and wondered what you were up to,” she replied.

As the sky lightened up, bringing in dawn and withering the darkness away, Theron and Eirys woke up as well. The four prepared themselves for the new day and with their belongings strapped securely to their backs, bid farewell to the warmth and comfort of Eirys' hut, setting out on the next leg of their journey.

The trail wound its way through the foothills, the rugged terrain challenging their every step. Luna led the way with unwavering determination, her knowledge of the land guiding them through rocky outcrops and dense foliage. Theron's keen eyes scanned their surroundings for any signs of danger, his hand never far from the hilt of his sword.

As they approached the entrance to the caverns, a sense of anticipation hung in the air. But their hopes were dashed as they beheld the sight before them - the entrance lay in ruins, buried beneath a mound of rubble and debris.

Frustration gnawed at them as they surveyed the damage, uncertain of their next move. It was Eirys who broke the silence, her voice tinged with uncertainty. "I know another path," she offered hesitantly, her brow furrowed in thought. "But it's not without its dangers. The mountain is home to many smaller monsters and beasts."

With no other options before them, the group made the difficult decision to press on, following Eirys as she led them along a treacherous path up the mountainside. The climb was grueling, each step bringing them closer to the unknown dangers that awaited them.

As they neared a small opening in the rocky face of the mountain, Eirys motioned for them to proceed with caution. "This is it," she whispered, her voice barely above a murmur. "The entrance to the caverns lies beyond."

But as they stepped inside, their footsteps echoing off the cavern walls, disaster struck in an instant. Without warning, a trap was triggered, and Alex felt himself being torn away from the group, his body engulfed in a blinding light.

When the light faded, Alex found himself alone with Eirys, the cavern stretching out before them in all directions. Panic seized him as he called out for Theron and Luna, but his cries were met with only silence. Somewhere deep within the darkness, a sense of foreboding stirred, and Alex knew that their journey had taken a dangerous turn.

As Alex and Eirys ventured deeper into the caverns searching for Luna and Theron, the darkness seemed to press in around them, swallowing up the faint glow of their torches. Every step was taken with caution, their senses alert for any sign of danger lurking in the shadows.

Once they felt assured that they weren't in any immediate danger, Eirys broke the silence, her voice echoing softly against the cavern walls. "Tell me about your world, Alex," she said, her tone curious. "What's it like where you come from? What do you miss the most?"

Alex paused, considering her question carefully. "My world... well, it's different from here," he began, his words slow and measured. "There are cities that stretch as far as the eye can see, filled with people from all walks of life. It's bustling and busy, always moving, always changing."

Eirys listened intently, her interest piqued. "And what do you miss the most about it?" she pressed, her voice soft with curiosity.

Alex's thoughts drifted back to his home, a pang of longing tugging at his heart. "I miss the simple things, I suppose," he admitted. "The sound of laughter, the smell of fresh-baked bread, the feeling of being surrounded by friends and family."

Eirys nodded in understanding, a hint of sadness flickering in her eyes. "It sounds like a beautiful place," she murmured, her voice barely above a whisper.

Turning the conversation back to Eirys, Alex asked about her life in the mountains. "Why do you choose to live out here alone?" he inquired, his curiosity getting the better of him.

Eirys smiled softly, a wistful look in her eyes. "The mountains hold many secrets, Alex," she replied cryptically. "They are abundant with herbs and plants that can be used for medicine and healing. And besides," she added with a playful glint in her eye, "I rather enjoy the solitude, although it never lasts for long - Luna and Theron always seem to find a way to pull me into their adventures."

As they continued to navigate the labyrinthine passages of the caverns, a subtle chemistry began to spark between them. For some reason, Alex found it much more comfortable talking to Eirys than Luna and Theron. Luna, as jestful and casual as she sometimes was, had an air of mystery around her. Theron, on the other hand, hardly talked when he didn't need to. With Eirys, Alex felt as if he could share more and hear more. It seemed like they understood each other much better.

The two continued with their conversation in whispers while still treading carefully. Eventually, they came across a huge block of door that seemed to be hiding something important behind it. They looked at each other before trying to push the door open. However, it was much too heavy for them to even make it budge. As Alex began racking his brain, trying to find a way they could make the door open, Eirys tapped his shoulder lightly and asked him to step back.

"This will help us," she said, holding a locket with a peculiar looking shard of blue gem attached to it. She whispered an incantation, holding the shard forward and suddenly, to Alex's surprise, the door flung open as if it had no weight at all. "That's awesome. What is that?" he inquired.

"It's a shard of the Crystal of Unsealing. It can open almost any kind of enclosements" Eirys replied.

The name instantly clicked with Alex as his memory went back to the time he had conversed with the Legendary Turtle. But before he could say another word, Alex's eyes froze as he looked past the huge door and saw what lay inside.

Chapter 6

A Close Shave

As Alex focused his gaze into the swirling darkness ahead, he couldn't help but be overcome with shock. There, amidst the suffocating grip of the shadowy mass, were what looked like roots. They didn't seem much unlike the intertwining and branching fabrics of reality that made up the Origin Tree that he had seen in his dream.

"Be careful, Alex," Eirys warned, her voice barely above a whisper. "There's something sinister lurking within that darkness."

Alex nodded, his gaze fixed on the swirling vortex of shadows.

"Are these... roots?" Alex whispered, his voice barely audible over the crackling energy surrounding them.

Eirys nodded solemnly, her eyes scanning the darkness with a mix of concern and dread. "Yes, but they're corrupted," she explained, her voice tinged with sorrow. "The roots of the Origin Tree are supposed to connect and distribute energies across the realms, but this...

this corruption is unlike anything I've ever seen."

The two slowly, but cautiously walked closer, trying to investigate the darkness. But as soon as they got closer, they were abruptly interrupted by the sudden appearance of a towering figure — a golem, its eyes glowing red with malevolent intent as it moved to intercept them.

"We need to get out of here," Alex urged, his heart pounding with urgency as he glanced toward the exit. But his hopes were dashed as he realized it was blocked, leaving them with no choice but to confront the monster almost twice his size.

Drawing out his determination, Alex stepped forward, his gaze locked on the approaching golem. "Stand back, Eirys," he instructed, his voice firm with resolve. "I'll handle this."

Focusing his mind and channeling his energy into his hands, Alex unleashed a burst of magical energy at the golem. However, to his dismay, it seemed to have little effect against the formidable foe.

Eirys watched anxiously from the sidelines, her heart pounding with every clash of magic. "You can do this, Alex," she encouraged, her voice filled with unwavering confidence.

Drawing upon his instincts and what Luna had taught him, Alex tried changing his approach. Instead of trying to overpower the golem with sheer force, he focused on finesse and precision, using his magic to manipulate the environment around him. With a flick of his wrist, he sent shards of rock hurtling toward the golem, aiming for its vulnerable joints and weak spots.

As the intense battle dragged on, each movement became a calculated dance of offense and defense. Alex and Eirys fought with unwavering determination, their attacks and dodges coming in rapid succession as they sought to weaken the formidable golem.

The golem's strikes were relentless, its massive fists crashing down with enough force to shatter stone. Alex managed to keep dodging it's fists, but a lack of fighting experience meant that he only had to make one mistake to get punched up in the air and thrown across the room.

"Alex!" screamed Eirys. She immediately began chanting her healing magic, trying to address the profuse bleeding of her partner.

There was no doubt in her mind that there were at least a few broken bones in his body, considering the force of the hit that he had just taken. But with Alex down and Eirys getting busy with chanting her incantation, she had become the prime target of the golem before she even realized.

"Eirys! Look back," Alex warned from where he laid.

Fortunately, her quick reflexes and agility built through years of training helped her narrowly escape its attacks. She deftly dodged its strikes, her magic weaving a protective barrier around her while still continuing her incantation until Alex had fulyl recovered.

As the battle wore on, the golem showed signs of weakening under the relentless assault. Sensing an opportunity, Alex decided to try something new. He focused his energy, channeling it into a powerful burst of flame that engulfed the golem.

"We've already tried using fire attacks... although now that it's weakened it does seem to be doing more damage," Eirys remarked, observing the effects of Alex's flames on the golem. But before she could finish her sentence, Alex followed up with another unexpected move—he summoned a blast of freezing cold, encasing the weakened golem in a shell of ice.

As the golem crumbled and fell apart almost instantly, Alex turned to Eirys with a triumphant grin. "Thermal shock," he explained, his voice filled with excitement. "I remembered reading about it and using it in one of my stories. I figured it might work. We're quite fortunate it did!"

But before they could catch their breath, however, a sudden explosion rocked the chamber, sending shockwaves rippling through the air. A portal opened before them, revealing a figure draped in black—a woman who exuded an aura of power and authority.

"I had to see for myself who destroyed my golem," the woman declared, her voice cold and calculating.

Alex's eyes narrowed as he faced the mysterious newcomer. "And who might you be?" he demanded, his tone defiant.

The woman shrugged dismissively. "Names are irrelevant," she replied cryptically. "But if you must know, you may call me Lilith."

Alex's mind raced with questions, but before he could voice them, Lilith confirmed his suspicions.

"Yes, I am responsible," she admitted, her gaze unwavering. "And I can't have you here trying to ruin my work."

Before Alex could respond, Lilith conjured another golem, even larger and more powerful than the last. With a sinister smirk, she vanished again through the portal, leaving Alex and Eirys to face the daunting challenge before them.

As Alex unleashed a barrage of attacks against the colossal golem, it became evident that his efforts were in vain. None of his strikes even fazed the towering creature. With a slow and deliberate movement, the golem activated, its massive form tensing as it prepared for a devastating attack.

With a forceful punch to the ground, the golem shattered the walls of the chamber they were inside, sending debris flying in all directions. Realizing the futility of fighting such a formidable foe, Alex shouted at Eirys to run, his voice echoing through the chaos.

"Run, Eirys! We can't fight this thing!" Alex yelled, urgency in his words as he grabbed her hand and guided her through the cracks in the crumbling walls.

Back in the caverns, they navigated their way through the winding passages, the sound of the golem's heavy footsteps echoing behind them. The two tried as hard as they could to put some distance between them, but the footsteps only seemed to draw in closer.

As they raced through the caverns, the golem's massive fist plunged towards Alex as it attempted to crush him. He only managed to narrowly avoid it thanks to Eirys, who pulled him out of range in time. Alex let out a huge sigh of relief as they both wasted no second to turn back and start running again.

Within a few seconds, the golem unleashed another powerful strike, this time picking up a rock and launching it towards them. Fortunately for them, they had managed to put some distance by then and it helped them dodge in time. The huge chunk of rock collided into the cavern wall, crumbling it enough to create a large hole that opened up to the foothills of the mountain. Without hesitation, Alex and Eirys accepted their stroke of luck and leaped through the opening, tumbling out into the open air as they landed amidst the rocky terrain.

Gasping for breath, they scrambled to their feet, their hearts pounding with adrenaline as they put as much distance as possible between themselves and the golem. As they glanced back at the mountain, they could see the massive creature looming in the darkness of the cavern, staring down at them with unrelenting malice before turning around and disappearing back into the shadows. For now, they were safe, since it didn't seem like it had any intention of chasing them further. They both knew they had narrowly escaped a fate far worse than they could have imagined.

A little while later, Luna and Theron arrived, their expressions a mix of concern and relief. Luna's eyes widened in alarm as she took in the disheveled appearance of Alex and Eirys, her worry palpable in the furrow of her brow.

"Alex! Eirys! Where were you guys?" Luna's voice was filled with genuine concern as she stepped closer, her gaze flickering between the two of them.

As Alex and Eirys recounted their harrowing ordeal, Luna's eyes widened with each detail, her concern deepening with every word. Alex noticed from her expression that she seemed to know something about this woman named Lilith. Theron listened intently, his face stern as usual, but also evidently weary. When Alex finished speaking, Theron let out a weary sigh, the weight of their recent trials evident in the slump of his shoulders.

"What happened with you two?" Alex's concern turned to Theron, his brow furrowing as he took in the exhaustion etched into his friend's features.

Theron shook his head wearily, a tired smile tugging at the corners of his lips. "Ugh, please don't ask," he replied, his voice heavy with exhaustion.

Luna chuckled softly, her amusement cutting through the tension that lingered in the air.

“Do you know about Dreamseekers, Alex?” she asked.

“Dreamseekers? You mean the little creatures who misguide people with illusions and make them hallucinate? I remember making them up for one of my stories,” he revealed.

“Well, they do exist here. Perhaps your link to our world helped you in your imagination. That’s quite... interesting,” she noted before returning back to the topic at hand. “Anyway, as it turns out, we were teleported deeper into the caverns," she began, her tone lightening as she recounted their own misadventures. "And then Theron here got caught up in a Dreamseeker's illusions and wouldn't stop attacking me. So, I had to use a little magic to knock some sense into him."

Theron nodded in agreement, his sheepish expression mirroring Luna's amusement. "It was... not my finest moment," he admitted, a hint of embarrassment coloring his words.

As they shared a moment of lighthearted laughter, the tension that had gripped them since their encounter with the golem began to dissipate slightly.

"Excuse me for a minute," Luna said, her tone gentle as she stepped away from the group, leaving Alex, Eirys, and Theron to wait for her return.

Alex turned to Eirys, his curiosity piqued by the shard she had used to open the door earlier. "That shard you used to open the door," he began, his voice filled with curiosity. "Where did you get it?"

Theron stood in silence, observing, as was his usual response to most situations that didn't require fighting.

Eirys glanced at the shard dangling from her necklace before meeting Alex's gaze. "A crow from the mountains gifted it to me when I saved it from a bear," she explained, her expression thoughtful. “Why do you ask?” she asked back.

Alex nodded, absorbing her words before he spoke again. "It’s because I'm looking for something called the Crystal of Unsealing," he revealed, his voice tinged with determination. "It’s what I need to free the Blue Turtle."

Eirys's eyes widened in surprise at his revelation. "I've heard of the Crystal of Unsealing," she replied, her voice contemplative. "But I heard it was broken into three shards. I have one and I’ve heard rumors of one being in the Capital. The third - I have no idea, "she added.

Alex's heart sank at the news, but he quickly composed himself, his resolve unwavering. "So, we'll need to find the other two shards," he concluded, his mind already racing with possibilities. "It seems my search just got harder - but not nearly enough to stop me from doing it. But for now, let’s focus on our current mission. Speaking of which - where’s Luna run off to?”

As Alex turned around to look for Luna, he saw her returning towards them. “She’s back,” Eirys noted.

"So, what do we do now about the darkness that's been infesting inside the caverns?" Alex asked, aiming towards Luna as she approached.

"I just communicated with the Elders of Echoes," she announced, her voice carrying a sense of urgency. "They want to hear about this infestation that's been corrupting the roots of the Origin Tree. I think we should consult with them first before we go back to take on the giant again."

Alex nodded in agreement. He had wanted to meet these "Elders" as well. They seemed important, and important people always have the answers. It's just a matter of how much they're willing to give to you and for what price.

"I agree, we should retreat for now," he suggested. "We'll gather our strength and return to take on that golem. But how do we get to consult him, Luna?" he ended with the question.

Alex imagined it would be something like a magic video call or perhaps a telepathic conversation. But without saying a word, Luna, with a wave of her hand, summoned a whirl of energy that enveloped all of them before teleporting them right in the presence of the Elders.

They found themselves standing in a vast chamber, its walls adorned with intricate carvings depicting the history of the realms. A soft glow emanated from the ceiling, casting an ethereal light over the room. As Alex looked around, he couldn't help but feel a sense of wonder. Regaining his composure, he turned to Luna and asked, “If you had the ability to teleport us, why didn’t you just teleport us to the Caverns? That would’ve saved us quite some time you know?”

“Ah! That was us, Alex.” One of the Elders seated in a circle at its center addressed him, his form and tone welcoming. Alex noticed their forms were obscured by robes of flowing fabric, each of them radiating an aura of ancient wisdom and power that seemed to permeate the very air around them. The one addressing him seemed to be the leader.

Theron and Eirys immediately bowed down before them, realizing who they were in the presence of. Luna stepped forward, her voice steady as she addressed the Elders. "We’ve returned, as you requested, Master Shoi." she announced, her tone respectful. “You did well, Luna,” he acknowledged her greeting before turning again towards Alex.

“Teleportation is quite a unique magic here in Echoes, Alex,” he explained. “It can only be used when your destiny requires you to. I request you not to fault Luna for it. I’m sure your journey so far has been arduos and we’ve invited you here because we want to hear more about it and possibly help in ways we can. But as you may have already realized, all of it has been guided by your own destiny.”

As Master Shoi continued on with his explanation of how teleportation worked here in Echoes, Alex couldn't stop himself from asking the question that gnawed at him all this time. "Was it you who brought me into this realm?" he ventured, his gaze fixed on the Elder's wise countenance.

Master Shoi nodded solemnly. "Indeed, Alex," he confirmed. "Your arrival here was no accident. Your destiny is intertwined with the fate of Echoes, and we believed you to be the key to restoring balance to our world."

“Huh! I would ask you why me, but I’m sure you’d just say it was destiny or something like that,” Alex seemed like he had come to accept these vague answers by now. It didn’t particularly change their plans in any way – he was still here and he still needed to do what was destined of him - but at least he learned who brought him here.

With a deep breath, Alex began recounting his and Eirys' recent encounter in the caverns, detailing the corruption that had threatened the roots of the Origin Tree. He looked to the Elders hoping that they would know what the clouds of darkness that they had seen were.

The Elders exchanged a knowing glance before Master Shoi spoke again. "The corruption you witnessed is the work of a powerful entity known as the Shadowweaver," he explained gravely. "It is a being of immense darkness, drawing its power from the realm of darkness, Dusk, to spread chaos and destruction."

Alex's brow furrowed with concern as he considered the implications of this revelation. "What about the woman in black?" he inquired, his voice tinged with urgency. "Do you know anything about her?"

To his surprise, Master Shoi's expression darkened with recognition. "Ah, Lilith," he murmured, his voice heavy with regret. "I had a feeling she might have been involved in this. Lilith is a formidable sorceress who has long dabbled in the powers of the realm of darkness.

She is cunning and dangerous, and her motives are shrouded in mystery."

Alex's mind raced with questions, but before he could voice them, Master Shoi continued. "Luna's knowledge of Lilith is not surprising," he explained. "They have had quite a history between them. But now that Lilith has revealed herself, we must tread carefully. She poses a threat not only to Echoes but to the fabric of reality itself."

With a heavy heart, Alex absorbed the Elder's words, knowing that their journey was far from over. “So, what do we do next?” he asked.

“We will get to that. But first, you must get some rest. I’m sure your friends would appreciate it as well. In the meantime, we will discuss among ourselves what our best course of action right now would be,” Master Shoi asserted.

Chapter 7

The Elders of the Citadel

As Luna led them out of the chamber, they found themselves stepping into a magnificent palace, its grandeur beyond anything Alex had ever seen before. The corridors were lined with towering pillars adorned with intricate carvings, while lush gardens bloomed with vibrant flowers and exotic plants. Fountains gurgled softly, their soothing melodies filling the air with a sense of tranquility.

"What is this place called?" Alex asked, his voice filled with wonder. Luna smiled warmly. "This is the Citadel," she replied. "It serves as the seat of power for the Elders and is located in the Capital of Echoes."

Alex's eyes widened in awe as he took in the splendor of the palace, his senses overwhelmed by the sheer beauty of his surroundings. Theron and Eirys seemed unfazed, having visited the place on numerous occasions before.

They accepted the hospitality of the Citadel, refreshing themselves before regrouping to explore the capital at Luna's suggestion. Stepping out into the streets of the Capital, Alex was greeted by a vibrant sight of the people of Echoes carrying on with their daily, busy lives. Market stalls lined the cobblestone streets, their wares ranging from exotic spices to shimmering magical artifacts.

As they wandered through the bustling thoroughfares, Alex's gaze fell upon an antique shop reminiscent of the one where he had purchased the Box of Echoes, the huge glowing board of "ANTIQUE" on top of the shop making it unmistakable. Intrigued, he stepped inside, the familiar jingle of bells announcing his arrival. Eirys and Theron joining him inside as well.

The shopkeeper greeted him warmly, his eyes twinkling with a knowing glint. He bore a striking resemblance to the shopkeeper from before, yet there was something different about him. "Welcome, traveler," the shopkeeper said, his voice echoing with wisdom. "Are you the same person who sold me the Box of Echoes?" Alex couldn't help but ask.

The shopkeeper looked initially with a keen expression, and then explained, "Oh! That must have been one of my brothers. We all operate the same shop, but across various timelines and realms. You must be Alex, right?

I've heard of you and your destiny from them. Wait a minute for me."

The shopkeeper disappeared behind the counter for a minute, leaving Alex to ponder what he was about. After a while, he appeared right back, producing a velvet-wrapped item. "I have been saving this for you, Alex. It will no doubt aid you on your journey," he said.

Curious, Alex inquired about the cost of the item, only to be met with a surprising response. "For you, Alex, it is free," the shopkeeper replied, his smile enigmatic. "Take it. You'll need it."

Accepting the item with gratitude, Alex tried to decide if he should ask more about this item – what it was and what it was supposed to do. But just then, Luna barged in through the door, interrupting his train of thought. "The Elders have called, Alex. It seems like they have reached a consensus," she announced.

With a nod of farewell to the shopkeeper, they made their way back to the Citadel. Back at the chamber of the Elders, Alex noticed that the Elders seemed a bit restless and at unease.

"Is everything alright, Master Shoi? What's our next plan of action?" he inquired.

“Welcome back, Alex. I hope you had a good tour of our Capital - although if you decide to explore it further, I’ll be happy to be your guide next time,” Master Shoi suggested with an inviting smile before he continued. “But for now, we unfortunately have far greater things to deal with. There’s been a new development - one that does not favor our cause.”

“We have received word of another corruption spreading in the distant reaches of Echoes - in the faraway Land of Lost Tales. It seems our work is far from over," he explained further. “Since Lilith discovered that we are already working to deal with the corruption, I assume she’s preparing contingency plans now.”

"What can we do to help, Master Shoi?" Luna asked, a grave look on her face.

“You must find and confront the sorceress, Lilith, and ask her about her intentions. We must learn what her motive is behind this corruption. But for now, you’ll need to deal with the corruptions themselves before they become even more dangerous,” Master Shoi replied before continuing. “Alex, Eirys, Theron, you have all shown great courage and determination in the face of adversity. Now, it is time to hone your skills further to be able to encounter and triumph over the threats that you'll encounter in your quest."

"What do you mean, Master Shoi?" Alex asked in his curiosity.

"I will impart to you advanced magic techniques, ones that will aid you in your quest to rid our realm of this darkness," Master Shoi explained before closing his eyes and waving his hands to summon a wave of energy from around him. The cloud of energy moved to envelop Alex, Theron, and Eirys before vanishing into thin air, transferring the energy from the Elder onto the other three.

“You should be able to use certain new spells now, Alex. You'll find them out by yourself when the time comes. As for Theron and Eirys, you two already possess specialized abilities. My blessings will surely enhance those abilities in combat,” he added.

"Thank you, Master Shoi. We won't let you down," Eirys said graciously on behalf of everyone, acknowledging the help they just received.

"Good. Now, before you depart, there is one more ally I wish to entrust to your care," Master Shoi continued.

"An ally? What do you mean?" inquired Theron, who had been observing silently, having barely spoken a word until now.

Master Shoi: "Dracy, you may enter."

As a short, child-like figure appeared from behind the doors, scales covering its skin like jewels embedded, Luna exclaimed, "A dragonling! How wonderful! It's a pleasure to meet you, Dracy."

"Thank you all for having me. I hope I'll prove to be useful to your quest. I understand that a lot is at stake here, and I want to do my best to save the world we live in," she replied, her voice bubbling with excitement.

"This little one will no doubt prove invaluable on your journey. Take care of it, and it will guide you through the trials ahead," said Master Shoi before bidding them farewell to let them continue their journey once again. "Farewell, travelers. And good luck!" he added before conjuring another portal to send them back in.

"Farewell to you too, and thank you for your help and care," Alex expressed his gratitude for the incredible hospitality they found in the Citadel before following Luna and the others through the portal.

Alex and his group found themselves standing right in front of the opening that Alex and Eirys had previously escaped from. Preparing themselves for a difficult fight, the five made their way in. Inside the caverns, their footsteps echoing in the dimly lit corridors, the tension in the air was palpable. Theron led the way, his sword drawn and his senses on high alert. Alex followed closely behind, his mind focused on the upcoming battle, while Eirys, Dracy, and Luna walked keeping their eyes open for attacks from the back, their magic at the ready.

As they entered the chamber once again, they were met with the imposing figure of the golem as it stood guard over the corrupted roots of the Origin Tree. Theron wasted no time, charging forward with a fierce battle cry as he engaged the golem in combat.

"Keep it distracted, Theron! I'll cover you from range," said Alex, his voice filled with determination.

"For Echoes!" Theron exclaimed, charging forward with his sword raised high. He swung his blade with fierce determination. However, the golem's thick armor proved to be a formidable defense, and his initial attacks glanced off harmlessly. The golem wasted no second in striking him back, sending him flying in the air.

Eirys reassured him from the back, casting her healing magic right away. Her eyes focused on the unfolding battle, she shouted, "I've got your back, Theron. Stay strong." Her soothing energy enveloped him, easing the pain and bolstering his resolve as he prepared to reengage the golem.

Meanwhile, Alex and Dracy engaged the monster with a flurry of magical attacks, weaving between its strikes with what agility had developed through each of their previous fights. Each spell they cast was aimed with precision, targeting the golem's vulnerable spots to maximize damage. Alex used the elemental magic that he had learned during his training with Luna, and Dracy used dragon-magic that was unique to her kin to slowly weaken the golem. The golem's defense was formidable, but Alex and Dracy's relentless assault began to wear it down, gradually bringing down its strength and speed.

"I'll focus on purifying the corruption from the roots," Luna declared, her magic already beginning to weave through the air.

As Theron recovered from the blow, he once again charged into the fray, this time readjusting his strategy. He stood still for a second and drew his powers, holding his sword in his hand as his magic began transforming it into a mace, a weapon he deemed more suited for this fight. He delivered blow after blow incessantly to the golem and with each strike, he slowly kept chipping away at the golem's armor.

Alex and Dracy continued providing ranged support as Eirys stood in some distance, providing support magic and healing to the ones in front. As Luna focused her efforts on dispelling the darkness that shrouded the roots of the Origin Tree, she noted, "The corruption is strong, but I can sense it weakening. Keep pressing on, we can do this!"

"I won't let up until this thing is dust," Theron vowed, his strikes relentless as he clashed with the golem.

“Yeah! We’ll beat it to dust!” Dracy joined in, her expression almost too cheerful as she continued her flashy dragon-magic attacks.

As the battle raged on, the golem proved to be a formidable opponent, its massive form shrugging off their attacks with ease. But with Theron continuing to pummel it with relentless force, and Alex and Dracy repeatedly targeting its weak points, cracks began to form in its exterior, finally giving them a sign that victory was within their grasp.

"Now's our chance! Luna, keep up the good work," Alex urged, seizing the opportunity to launch a fresh assault.

With a surge of determination, Alex tapped into the magic bestowed upon him by the Elder, summoning forth creatures from the stories he had written. From the depths of his imagination emerged a Dreamseeker and a Bull-dozer, a creature that's known for its incredible ramming power. Their forms shimmered with ethereal energy as they joined the fray.

"Let's see how you like this, you oversized tin can," Alex exclaimed, ordering his summons to attack the threat in front of them.

The Dreamseeker immediately cast a magic on the golem that caused it to lose its senses and start attacking randomly in any direction. Using this confusion to the advantage, the Bull-dozer charged, it's heavy and bovine figure building up incredible momentum. With speed and force, the Bull-dozer channeled it's charge right where the golem had started to develop cracks.

Finally, Dracy started building up her special attack. "Stand back everyone," she warned as she began taking a huge breath. Once she was done, she let out a breath of lava with incredible speed, pushing through the cracks of the golem's armor and flowing inside it.

Their combined efforts proved to be too much for the golem to withstand. With a final, thunderous roar, the golem collapsed to the ground, its form crumbling into dust. The Dreamseeker and the Bull-dozer disappeared and soon after, the darkness that had plagued the roots of the Origin Tree also began dissipating into thin air as Luna managed to succeed in her task. "We did it! The corruption is gone," Luna announced, a note of triumph in her voice.

"Well fought, everyone. We make a formidable team," Theron acknowledged, his gaze sweeping over his companions with pride.

"Our work is far from over yet," Eirys said as the group exited the caverns from the same opening, her expression serious as she contemplated their next steps. "There's still another one of these corruption that we need to attend to and make sure doesn't get out of hand. But for now," she said, relaxing her expression a bit, "I guess we stand victorious!"

"Ah... Now that you mention it, I feel like I'm done walking around from one corner of this world to another. Isn't there a better way we can reach the Land of Whatever-it-was?" Alex asked Luna, a look of exhaustion already washing over his face.

"The Land of Lost Tales, Alex," Luna retorted. "About that - don't you worry!" Dracy interrupted them before Luna could speak another word.

As Alex watched first in interest, then in awe and wonder, Dracy's form transformed with magic, revealing her true nature - a red-scaled fiery-looking dragon, one that looked like it had been summoned straight from one of the fantasy books that Alex had written. "Get on! We're going for a ride," Dracy said in her dragon form.

As Theron, Luna, Eirys, and Alex climbed up on her back with her permission, Dracy began flapping her wings with enough power to generate huge clouds of dust from where they stood.

"Woohoo!" she shouted, generating enough lift to carry all of them up high into the air.

Chapter 8

The Land of Lost Tales

As the group soared through the sky, the landscape below changed dramatically, and Alex couldn't help but marvel at the sights below. The view below kept changing with patches of forest, dry land, and civilization coming and going one after another. Eventually, as they covered some distance, he noticed a grand palace shining in white and gold surrounded by a huge chunk of land dotted with buildings that resembled the ones he had seen in the Capital. He turned to Luna with a questioning look. "Is that the Citadel?" he asked.

Luna nodded. Yes, it is. But I'm surprised you were able to make it out from up here. "I've always had great eyesight," Alex said in a joking tone.

Dracy joined in the conversation, her excitement palpable. "I can't wait to finish the mission and go back to the capital to have some dumplings! Have you ever had them, Alex?" she asked eagerly, her eyes gleaming with anticipation. Alex shook his head. "No, I haven't."

Dracy grinned. "Well, you're in for a treat! I promise to take you to eat dumplings together after this."

Alex chuckled, the thought of savory dumplings filling his mind with anticipation. "I'll hold you to that," he replied, a smile cornering his lips.

After about half a day of flying, they reached a quaint village nestled near the Land of Lost Tales. As they descended from the sky, Dracy's form shifted back into her human-like shape, her fiery wings retracting as they touched down near the village. Luna turned to the group, her expression earnest. "Perhaps we should inquire with the locals about the corruption troubling their land," she suggested.

Nodding in agreement, they approached the villagers, who greeted them with a mixture of weariness and hope.

"We didn't think anyone would come to save us," one villager confessed, their voice tinged with resignation.

Alex's brow furrowed in confusion. "But why would you think that?" he asked, genuinely curious.

The village head stepped forward, his weathered face reflecting the weight of centuries-old sorrow and determination. “I am Kline, the village chief,” he introduced himself.

Kline began explaining the tragic history of their once-prosperous kingdom, and how it came to be known as the Land of Lost Tales. Kline's narrative painted a vivid picture of their flourishing kingdom centuries ago when it was renowned for its vibrant culture, thriving arts, and rich heritage. Its cities were bustling hubs of commerce and culture, where merchants traded goods from distant lands, artists showcased their masterpieces, and scholars delved into the mysteries of the universe.

The kingdom was known for its architectural marvels, with towering palaces adorned with intricate carvings and colorful mosaics, and grand temples dedicated to the gods. The streets bustled with life, lined with bustling markets, lively taverns, and theaters where performers entertained the masses with tales of heroism and adventure.

The people of the kingdom were known for their hospitality and generosity, welcoming travelers from far and wide with open arms. Festivals and celebrations filled the calendar, honoring the changing seasons, the harvest, and the gods who watched over them.

"But all that changed with the Incident of the Lost Tales a few hundred years ago," Kline continued, his voice heavy with emotion. "When the Origin Tree's root that flows beneath us exploded and created the abyss, it consumed almost all traces of our history in the darkness that followed."

"We were forgotten, lost to the annals of time," he explained, his words carrying the weight of centuries of sorrow. "We feared that this time, the corruption would erase us completely from existence. But now, with your arrival, there is hope."

Alex and his group listened intently, hoping they would find some clues as to why all of this was happening from his stories. After he was done, Kline expressed heartfelt gratitude on behalf of the village to Alex and his companions, offering them a reward if they could rid their land of the corruption that threatened to consume them.

"Of course, we will definitely get rid of this corruption," Alex assured him. "We've already taken care of one in the Caverns of Shadows."

"That's very reassuring," Kline replied. "We'll hope for your success and safe return.

And if you're able to achieve your mission, we'll forever be in your debt, Alex."

With a renewed sense of purpose and determination, Alex and the others, guided by the village head, set out towards the abyss located a few miles from the village, where the corruption supposedly was. As Alex and the others approached the edge of the abyss, they gazed down into its depths, where the bottom was shrouded in darkness, rendering it invisible.

"You know, the abyss might be looking back at us right now," Eirys joked, noting that they were all staring right into it. Dracy, ever the instigator, teased Eirys, "Are you afraid, little healer?"

Eirys shook her head with a grin. "Not when I have a fiery dragon like you to protect me," she retorted, her tone laced with playful banter.

For a brief second, disappointment washed over Dracy's face as she realized that Eirys wasn't letting her provocation get to her. "Fine!" she said. "I guess I'll have to save you all if the time comes," a huge smile adoring her face once again.

Assured by Dracy's reassurance that she could transform into her dragon form to whisk them to safety if needed, the group exchanged determined glances before taking a collective leap of faith and plugging into the depths of unknown below. As they neared the surface underground, Luna's magic cushioned their descent, softening the impact as they landed on the rocky floor below. “It’s so dark,” Theron noted quietly. “I can hardly see anything.”

“Don’t you worry, I’ve got it!” Dracy exclaimed before illuminating their path by casting a ball of light using her powers that led their way. The journey forward was fraught with peril, with monstrous creatures lurking in the shadows. Unlike their journey until now, it was clear that there was a clear intention to keep them from reaching their goal. As the group proceeded through the dark void of the abyss, their fight continued with these monsters springing onto them from every corner one after another. Fortunately, with the Master Shoi’s blessing, the group didn’t have much difficulty sustaining themselves against them.

As they progressed further, they soon reached another set of doors deep within the abyss – one that was strangely similar to the ones they had discovered in the caverns. Eirys stepped forward once again, her crystal shard glinting in the dim light as she used it to unlock the doors, revealing a similar chamber within which the root of the Origin Tree lay corrupted by the ominous dark clouds that was swirling all over it.

This time, they were prepared for a tougher fight. But what they failed to predict was that this time, their opponent was much, much more formidable than they had imagined. There were no golems or monsters around within the chamber. Instead, before them stood Lilith herself, her figure bathed in darkness, her eyes gleaming with malevolent intent.

“Welcome, I have been waiting for you,” she declared in a chilly voice, clearly intending conflict. “Before you challenge me, however,” she continued, “I must warn you to be prepared to put your lives on the line. “

Alex met her gaze with unwavering resolve. "We've been putting our lives on the line since the moment we embarked on this journey," he declared, his voice steady despite the rising tension. "And we're not about to back down now."

“Very well then,” said Lilith before using her magics to summon a dark silhouetty figure, one that Alex and the others knew quite well.

"I assume you were the one who sent this Skavari to us then, Lilith?" Luna asked, her voice more authoritative now.

"Oh, hey Luna!" Lilith quipped. "I didn't even see you there. But yes, you're right. Master Alteoth believed that you were going to be a hindrance to our plan. So, he asked me to send him after you. Too bad, he was too weak to carry out his mission. But don't worry – he's had plenty of time to get stronger, thanks to my powers of darkness."

"Alteoth?" Alex asked, curiosity gripping him strongly. Was his dream real after all? Was it a dream at all? Was everything that he saw real?

Realizing that she had spoken more than she wanted to, Lilith gestured at the Skavari, instructing him to launch his attack. In an instant, the Skavari appeared next to Theron and slashed through his garb. If Theron hadn't seen it coming and dodged it, he had no doubt that he would have sustained injuries much graver.

There was no doubt in anyone's mind that the Skavari had become much stronger than the last time they encountered each other. Knowing that it could be risky to let him change his target, Theron pushed in with a counter attack. But the Skavari deflected his blade with ease and would've launched another attack at Theron if not for Alex who distracted him with his magic. While Alex and Theron had their hands full trying to keep up with the Skavarian, Eirys took the opportunity to start casting healing magic on both of them to prevent them from sustaining major damages.

"Thanks, Eirys," Alex acknowledged her efforts even as he kept dodging the Skavarian's attacks.

Meanwhile, Dracy and Luna turned their attention to Lilith, launching their own attacks one after another. Unfortunately for them, none of their attacks seemed to work as Lilith effortlessly deflected every single one of them. "Damn! Her defense is impenetrable," Dracy shrieked.

"Don't worry, I have a plan," Luna said, trying to keep up her motivation as they continued their attacks seemingly in vain. She signalled Dracy to change positions, both of them trying to corner Lilith as they now focused on a pincer attack strategy. Luna channeled her light magic from one side as Dracy used her dragon magic from the other.

"You really sure you want to fight me again, Luna?" Lilith asked, still blocking and deflecting all of their attacks. "Don't you remember what happened the last time you tried to?"

"Your provocations only tell me that you're scared, Lilith," Luna retorted, focusing on her magic to try and get some damage in.

"Ha! You're only so good with your words, Luna. If only your magic was as good!" Lilith continued their battle banter when suddenly, a crushing force from behind her sent her flying forward.

"You should really focus more on your surroundings!" Alex joined in their banter just then.

Shocked and baffled, as Lilith got back up from the ground to see what had attacked her, she realized that there was a Bull-dozer staring right at her. Looking over to the other side when Theron was fighting with the Skavarain, she realized what had just happened.

Alex had used his powers to summon the Dreamseeker and the Bull-dozer. While the Dreamseeker kept the Skavarian busy with its illusions, Alex has targeted the Bull-dozer at Lilith to help out Luna and Dracy.

"No one said this wasn't a team fight," Alex laughed out, noticing the look on Lilith's face.

As Alex's group regained their fighting morale at the first breakdown of the unbeatable opponent, Lilith's rage made sure they got back on their toes really fast.

"Arrgh!" shouted Lilith as she released her magic, the Skavarian vanishing again into thin air. "I see that I'll have to take all of you on by myself. But so be it. Master Alteoth should probably already be ready for the next move by now. I have to make this quick." Who's Alteoth? Alex finally managed to ask.

"You don't need to know about that. But if you do want to know, know that all of your lives are already on the countdown. Master Alteoth will do anything to achieve his goal," Lilith shared. She then raised her arms, chanting a spell and covering herself in a shroud of darkness.

"Stand back," Theron immediately warned the others. "This is going to be a very difficult fight." Theron may have warned others, but every one of them had already felt it in their bones that before them stood something far more powerful than they had imagined they would be fighting.

With a swift move, Lilith launched a myriad of attacks toward Alex and his group. By the time they had barely managed to dodge her attacks, Lilith had already charged her next series of attacks.

"We're clearly outmatched!" shouted Eirys as she jumped and pranced around trying to dodge the attacks. "We must fight together as one!" Theron roared. "Only then do we stand a chance."

Theron was definitely the most experienced one amongst their group when it came to combat. So, hearing him say this, the others regained their fighting spirit, noting that it was still a fight they were capable of winning if they played their cards right. "We need a formation," Luna exclaimed.

But just then, as if reading her opponents perfectly, Lilith summoned five new monsters. Clad in black and bowing down to Lilith, it was clear that these monsters were in a different league than any of her previous summons.

"They're my personal bodyguards," Lilith explained with a smirk. "I hope you'll put up a good fight because these boys like to have fun."

The fight once again gained momentum as this time, Alex and the others truly felt outnumbered and outmatched, trying to handle all the monsters and Lilith herself. Desperately trying to find a way out of their current predicament, Alex racked his brain intensely until he came up with a plan. It was a simple plan, and its success was unassured. Nevertheless, realizing that it was a matter of life and death, Alex decided to take on the gamble. “Guys, stick together!” he hollered at the others.

The five huddled together at Alex’s instructions, making Lilith’s bodyguards chase them into a circle. As soon as they had gotten close enough, Alex first gestured Dracy and then weaved his hands together, summoning another being - this time a giant that stood taller than all of them, a huge club in his hand that it used to ravage villages in his stories. Alex was glad that this time, the giant was on their side.

“Meet my bodyguard,” Alex looked straight at Lilith and let out a smile before signaling his intent to the giant. With one huge swing of his club, the giant cracked open the ground, revealing a gaping pit that stretched down below to the heart of the abyss.

Reading his plans, Dracy immediately assumed her dragon form, carrying Alex, Luna, Eirys, and Theron on her back as Lilith’s bodyguards plunged into the darkness below by themselves.

Chapter 9

A Night at Kline's

With Lilith's bodyguards dispatched and the focus squarely on the dark sorceress herself, Alex and his companions steeled themselves for the final confrontation. The chamber crackled with an intense energy, the air thick with anticipation as they prepared to face their greatest challenge yet.

Luna, the master of light magic, stood at the forefront, her eyes ablaze with determination. With a graceful motion of her hands, she unleashed torrents of radiant energy, each spell weaving through the air like shimmering threads of light. The brilliance of her magic dazzled and disoriented Lilith, forcing the sorceress to shield herself from the blinding onslaught. Luna's spells danced around Lilith, closing off avenues of escape and leaving her vulnerable to the group's coordinated assault.

Theron, the stalwart warrior, charged into battle with a fierce determination. His sword gleamed in the dim light of the chamber as he clashed with Lilith's summoned creatures. With each swing of his blade, he kept them at bay, his movements a blur of precision and strength. Theron's skill with a sword was unmatched, and he carved through Lilith's defenses with relentless ferocity, his strikes landing true and deep.

Eirys, the gentle healer with a heart of gold, remained vigilant on the sidelines, her healing magic poised to aid her companions in their time of need. With whispered incantations, she sent waves of soothing energy washing over them, bolstering their resolve and replenishing their strength. Eirys' presence was a comforting beacon in the chaos of battle, her magic weaving a protective barrier around her allies as they pressed forward.

Dracy, the fiery dragon, soared through the air with grace and power, her wings beating rhythmically as she unleashed bursts of fiery breath upon Lilith's defenses. Each blast weakened the sorceress, leaving her vulnerable to their relentless onslaught. Dracy's mere presence was enough to instill fear in their enemy, her formidable strength and unwavering resolve a testament to her indomitable spirit.

As for Alex, he stood at the heart of the fray, his mind sharp and focused. Rather than using his summoning magic anymore, he focused on coordinating his attacks with those of his companions, maximizing their effectiveness. He switched back to more basic attacks and with precise gestures and timely maneuvers, he managed to help his teammates drive Lilith back with relentless force. His strategic mind was a valuable asset in the heat of battle, his keen intuition guiding their every move as they closed in on their elusive foe.

Lilith's powers were no doubt formidable, but the group fought with unwavering determination, each member complementing the others with their skills. With each strike and spell, they chipped away at Lilith's defenses, inching closer to victory with every passing moment.

But Lilith was cunning and resourceful, not one to go down without giving Alex's team a run for their money. With a snarl of rage, she unleashed a barrage of dark magic, her spells striking with deadly precision. The group stood firm, their resolve unshaken as they weathered her attacks and returned fire with equal ferocity. The air crackled with energy as the clash of magic and steel echoed through the chamber, each side refusing to yield an inch in the face of overwhelming odds.

As the battle raged on, the chamber seemed to shrink around them, the walls closing in as if to crush them under the weight of their struggle. But still, they fought on, their determination unyielding in the face of adversity. With each passing moment, the tide of battle shifted back and forth, neither side willing to give ground as they fought tooth and nail for victory.

Finally, it seemed like Alex and the others had managed to corner Lilith and weakened her enough under their relentless assault. Victory seemed within their grasp, but before they could deliver the final blow, she let out a final cry and channeled her magic all around her. Alex and the others cautioned themselves as they took a step back, not knowing what to expect. But as soon as they put some distance, Lilith said, "I may have underestimated your ragtag group of heroes, Luna. But the Origin Tree should be weakened enough by now. You should count your days and spend it more wisely than trying to chase me down or trying to stop us."

She then summoned a swirl of darkness and disappeared right into it, escaping their grasp.

Confused, Alex turned to Luna. "How can she teleport like that and we have to let destiny do it for us?" he asked, his brow furrowed in puzzlement.

Luna sighed, her expression grave. "She's using dark magic," she explained. "It's forbidden within Echoes, but Lilith has always been reckless. More importantly, however, judging from what she said, I fear she might have more sinister plans regarding the Origin Tree. We need to find out what her goals are exactly."

"I think I may have an idea about what she wants," Alex said, his mind reflecting back on the dream that he seemed to remember so vividly.

Luna asked Alex to explain what he meant by that, but Alex resisted. "I know we're teammates and I trust you with my life after all we've been through, but right now, I want to talk about it with the Elders first. I have a few questions myself that I want answers to," he said.

"I understand," Luna replied, accepting the fact that Alex probably had some good reason for his decision. "Let's tend to the corruption first, then we can make our way back to the Citadel," she continued, noting that they had yet to address the problem that they came for in the first place.

As Alex and the others stood in guard, making sure they were ready to deal with any unexpected attacks, Luna got to work and started purging the corruption from the root of the Origin Tree. It took a while, as Lilith had woven in snares and traps into her magic to deter their efforts. But eventually, Luna managed to remove the clouds of darkness, thanks to her light magic which worked naturally against the darkness.

As the last traces of the corruption dissipated, the surrounding landscape seemed to come alive with newfound vitality. The air, once heavy with darkness, now felt crisp and pure, infused with the rejuvenating magic of Echoes. A sense of tranquility settled over the group, their weary spirits uplifted by the knowledge that they had succeeded in their mission.

Fighting a few more hordes of monsters as they exited the chamber, Alex and the others eventually managed to get out of the abyss. Finally, they returned to the village, greeted by the warm embrace of its grateful inhabitants.

"Alex! We're glad to see you again. How did your journey through the abyss turn out?" Kline asked him as soon as he spot him.

Alex recounted their journey into the abyss, his words painting a vivid picture of the challenges they had overcome and the victory they had achieved. The villagers listened intently, their expressions a mix of relief and gratitude as they realized that the immediate threat they had been worrying about had been averted.

Kline, the village head, however, expressed his concern at the revelation of Lilith's involvement. “She’s an evil one,” he said. “I’ve heard from my predecessors that she was the one responsible for that incident. It’s shocking… And, honestly, terrifying to hear that she’s still alive and back again. But for now you have our deepest gratitude, Alex. You and your friends have saved our village from certain doom, and for that, we are eternally grateful."

“We were only doing what we were here to do, Kline,” Alex replied, trying to be courteous. “We’re grateful to you as well for the information you provided us. If not for you, it could have taken us much more time and we would probably have spent much more energy trying to figure out our path inside the abyss.”

“Well, now that it’s all done - at least for now - how about we have some food and drinks together? The villagers want you to spend the night here. Some of them are really keen on hearing your stories from other adventures,” Kline proposed, glancing at the two children standing besides him with a curious look on their faces. “These are my kids, Lela and Mikel.

They've been really looking forward to your return so that they could hear your stories again," Kline introduced them to Alex.

"Thank you so much for your gestures but I think we should be hurrying back. We never know when Lilith is going to strike again, but when she does, we must be ready," Alex replied. His face adorned a smile as he waved at the kids, but the stress behind his expression was clear to every adult present there. "Lela, Mikel, I promise you we'll be back. And then Uncle Alex will bring you many, many more stories from where I come from!" he tried explaining to them.

"Uh... Alex. I feel like I'm too tired to travel anywhere right now - that fight had me drained!" Eirys said, standing behind with an obviously fake limp. "Maybe we should take up on their offer and rest. I doubt Lilith would be in any better shape than us right now," she continued as her sly smile made it clear that she had every intention of staying there for a while and giving the kids what they wanted.

Alex thought about it a while, knowing that Lilith wasn't the only one they should be worried about. However, after taking a look at his teammates' faces, he hesitantly agreed.

"Fine," he conceded. "But we set off from here at the first sight of dawn."

With the feeling of celebration spreading around among the villagers, Alex's friends wasted no time in getting into the mood themselves. Kline wholeheartedly invited them to the local village pub. The group spent the rest of the evening engaging in the comforting foods and delicious ale that the village took pride in. After answering some curious villagers' questions and getting to know more about the people, it was finally time for them to get some rest. Kline again invited them over, this time to his house, and asked them to stay the night there. "I've already made preparations for you. Lela and Mikel helped set the beds!" he informed them, a hint of a doting father's excitement in his voice.

Alex and the others gladly accepted his invitation and together they made their way from the pub to Kline's house. It was a modest hut, one that had the marks of having been repaired time and time again. "Come in," he guided them. Contrary to the looks of it, Alex and his friends were almost surprised at how spacious it was inside. There were separate rooms and quite a large living room in the center of the hut.

Eirys, Luna, and Dracy had one room to themselves while Alex and Theron stayed in another. Kline gave them a short tour of the hut on the way in and showed them the rooms they would be staying in. As they all entered their respective rooms and Alex found himself being carried away by Lela and Mikel instead, who were eagerly waiting for Uncle Alex's stories.

After sharing a few stories from his home as he promised, as the children took to bed, Alex found himself alone with Kline for a moment. He couldn't help but ask him something that had been on his mind.

"I hope you don't mind me asking, Kline, but I noticed that it's only you three living here," he asked.

"You're quite observant, Alex," Kline replied with a smile that looked like it had been hiding years of pain. "Lela and Mikel lost their mother a few years back. She had been sick for a while before that," he added, his face almost turning grim.

"I'm sorry, I shouldn't have asked," Alex replied, his voice reflecting the gravity of the situation.

"Oh, no. It's fine. The past few years have been devastating for me, but I have now learned to find strength in the wellbeing of my children. I'm sure Leona would have wanted this as well," said Kline, forcing himself to bring back the smile once again. "You should get some rest. I'll be right in the next room in case you need me for anything!" he said and with a pat of gratitude on Alex's shoulder, left him to get the rest that they very much deserved and needed.

"I will," Alex resonated with Kline's feeling before retiring into his room to find Theron already having made himself comfortable.

The golden rays of sunlight seeping in through the window woke Alex up gently the next morning. Theron was already up and almost ready.

"Weren't you the one who suggested leaving at dawn?" Theron asked him, his question blatantly exuding his taunting intentions.

"Ah-" Alex slowly pulled himself up and looked over towards Theron before dismissing him and focusing on making himself leave the bed. "It's not my fault these beds are so comfortable," he quipped as he hung his legs down.

After freshening themselves up and having a light breakfast, as the group was about to take their leave, Kline asked them for a minute. “I made a promise of a reward to you and your friends, Alex. And since you’ve done your part, I must do mine,” he said.

He then gestured to Mikel, who instantly dashed into Kline’s room and came back with a velvet wrap in his hand. He handed it to Kline, who in turn handed it to Alex. As Alex unwrapped the piece of velvet in his hands, his face shone up with excitement. His eyes widened in astonishment at what lay before him. It was another shard of the Crystal of Unsealing, the very artifact he had been searching for to free the Blue Turtle. His heart swelled with gratitude as he accepted the precious gift, realizing that Kline had unknowingly aided him in his quest.

"Thank you, Kline," Alex said sincerely, his voice filled with emotion. "You've made our journey a little easier."

Kline nodded, a smile spreading across his weathered face. "It was the least I could do," he replied humbly. "You have done more for us than we could ever repay. You’re all welcome to our village if you wish to visit anytime!" he announced.

With two of the three shards of the Crystal of Unsealing in possession, Alex and his companions bid farewell to Kline and mounted Dracy's back once more as they set off for the Citadel.

Chapter 10

The Truth about the Dream

Back at the Citadel, Alex and his companions once again found themselves in the chamber of the Elders.

"Welcome Alex, Luna, Eirys, Theron, and Dracy. I see that you've returned well and sound. I presume your mission has been successful?" enquired Master Shoi as the other Elders sat silent looking intently.

As Alex described what happened inside the Abyss, the Elders' faces expressed a range of emotions. But Alex kept his question for until the end. Once he was done narrating what had happened, he asked, "Do you know anything about Alteoth?"

"Alteoth?" Master Shoi asked back with a look of confusion and concern at the mention of the name.

"I...uh. I have been having this dream. It seemed weirdly real, almost as if it was a vision instead of a dream," Alex confessed. He looked over to his teammates who seemed equally confused. He couldn't blame them either because he hadn't mentioned about this to any of them before now.

"Could you describe your dream to me as well, Alex? It seems like you have questions. Maybe I can help with them," Master Shoi replied.

As Alex recounted his dream to the Elders, a hushed silence fell over the chamber, broken only by the sound of his voice echoing off the stone walls. He narrated once again, detailing the person named Alteoth that he saw, his daughter, the Origin Tree, and the God-Designers. The Elders listened intently, their expressions reflecting intrigue and concern at the same time as the tale unfolded. Alex realized that there was a chance that this all backfired, but it seemed like he had no choice. He needed answers and he knew this was his best chance to get them.

Master Shoi's brow furrowed in thought as he absorbed the details of Alex's dream. It was clear that the mention of Alteoth and the God-Designers struck a chord with him. He certainly knew something, and Alex hoped he would share his knowledge.

"The God-Designers..." Master Shoi began explaining. "They were beings of immense power, said to have shaped the very fabric of reality itself. But their influence waned long ago, and now they are little more than myths and legends."

"And as for Alteoth..." he trailed off for a second, before continuing. "The name is not unfamiliar to us," Master Shoi began, his voice tinged with solemnity. "He was once a revered figure among the God-Designers, a powerful sorcerer who possessed knowledge of magic beyond that of any other. But then he committed a sin against all his kin."

"You see, the God-Designers had a rule that they could never fall in love. As the males were destined to be the designers of realms and realities, so did their females have a predestined role – to become the vassals of the Origin Trees. Alteoth committed the sin of falling in love with his wife, Elana. And eventually, when his wife died in childbirth, Alteoth was banished and made a prisoner for eternity – or so we thought," Master Shoi's face suddenly turned grave.

"If what you speak is true, and it was indeed Alteoth's daughter who was sacrificed for the Origin Tree in Echoes, it might not be a stretch to conclude that he is back. And if he is, it would be obvious what he's here for – or rather, who," Master Shoi finally concluded.

"Assuming that Lilith is working for Alteoth, why would he intentionally corrupt the roots of the Origin Tree?" Alex posed another question towards him.

"I can only guess, but if I had to, I'd say that the corruptions probably weaken the connection of the Origin Tree with this realm of Echoes. Once weakened, he probably has some plan to uproot the Tree," Shoi explained. His eyebrows tensed as he continued, "What I don't understand, however, is why he would do that if he wants to save his daughter."

"Can we do anything to help him get his daughter back without disrupting the Origin Tree and Echoes?" Eirys asked, her expression empathetic and concerned. "It's sad enough that he lost his wife, and then they sacrificed his only daughter as well!"

Master Shoi nodded sideways. "The Origin Tree is vital to our realm, and more so, the reality as a whole since our realm acts as a medium for the threads of other realms. If he manages to uproot the Tree, it could spell doom for us all. There's one way, however, but it's probably not even worth discussing. I believe we should focus on stopping Alteoth altogether," he explained after careful consideration.

"What is this way you speak of? I think we should at least hear it before dismissing it completely," Alex protested against Master Shoi's judgement.

Shoi hesitated a little but looking at the eager faces of Alex and his friends, he spoke, "It has been noted in the ancient texts that the vassal of the Origin Tree can be replaced, but for that to happen, you'll need two things foremost – a being with a very high capacity for magic who shall take its place and another with an equally high capacity for magic who shall use his powers to conduct the ritual for the replacement and keep the threads of reality bound while the process is in place."

"How high are we talking about?" Luna, who had been listening to everything intently and silently up until now, asked.

"To be honest, neither of you nor even any one of us have the capacity that would be required. It's an incredibly complex and esoteric process that we're talking about. This is why I mentioned it wouldn't even be worth discussing," Master Shoi answered.

As the room fell silent once again with the inhabitants all working their own thoughts on it, Alex spoke once again, "I'd like to have some time before we decide to go after Alteoth to stop him. I have a feeling that I may be able to find a solution to this – or rather, know someone who might," he surmised, looking over at Master Shoi for his approval.

"If that's how you feel, I won't stop you, Alex. But remember, we don't have quite a lot of time. If we don't hurry, we might end up being too late to stop Alteoth," Shoi nodded, not wanting to turn Alex and his friends against their interest. I understand. I'll keep that in mind, Alex responded.

With the conversation at an end, Alex and his companions took their leave, their minds buzzing with thoughts and questions. It was clear that their journey was far from over, and that they carried heavy responsibilities on their shoulders. As they exited the chamber of the Elders, a tense silence hung in the air, punctuated only by the sound of their footsteps echoing off the stone walls.

"Alex," Luna began, her voice tinged with a hint of reproach. "Why didn't you tell us about your dream sooner? We're supposed to be a team, and keeping secrets from each other isn't going to help us in the long run."

Eirys nodded in agreement, her expression a mixture of disappointment and understanding. "We've been through so much together, Alex. We trust each other with our lives, so why wouldn't you trust us with something like this?"

Theron crossed his arms over his chest, his gaze fixed on Alex with a mixture of curiosity and concern. "I get that it's a lot to process, but we're all in this together. We need to be open and honest with each other if we're going to have any hope of stopping Alteoth."

Dracy, in her human-like form, remained silent, her eyes narrowed thoughtfully as she regarded Alex with a scrutinizing gaze. It was clear that she, too, was eager for an explanation.

Alex sighed, his shoulders slumping slightly under the weight of their combined scrutiny. "I'm sorry," he began, his voice tinged with regret. "I didn't mean to keep it from you. It's just... I didn't know what to make of the dream at first, and I didn't want to worry any of you unnecessarily."

Luna placed a comforting hand on Alex's shoulder, her expression softening with understanding. "We're not upset, Alex. We just want to make sure we're all on the same page moving forward. Whatever happens, we're here for you."

Eirys nodded in agreement, her eyes shining with sincerity. "You don't have to go through this alone, Alex. We're a team, remember?"

Theron clapped Alex on the back, a reassuring smile tugging at the corners of his lips. "We've faced worse than this before, mate. Together, there's nothing we can't handle."

“Thank you, everyone. It’s really reassuring to know you guys still have my back. I promise I’ll do what needs to be done,” Alex replied, breathing a sigh of relief.

Dracy nodded in silent agreement, her expression thoughtful as she contemplated their next move. “What next then?” she asked.

It seemed that despite the initial shock of Alex's revelation, they were all united in their determination to confront whatever challenges lay ahead. After all, all of their fates rested in Alex’s hands now and they knew they had to trust him.

“I want to talk to the Blue Turtle once before we go after Alteoth. I feel like it might have some insight for us that could prove to be usefu” Alex revealed his plan. “Dracy can you carry us to the village of Turtleblue?” he then asked.

"Of course," replied Dracy as she wasted no time transforming into her dragon form once they were outside. Once again, carrying all of them on her back, Dracy soared through the sky, this time heading for the village nestled by the lake where Alex first met the Blue Turtle.

As they reached the village of Turtleblue, nestled by the serene lake where Alex first encountered the Blue Turtle, a sense of anticipation hung in the air. Following Alex's directions, Dracy gracefully landed near the water's edge, her massive form dwarfing the surrounding landscape. With a gentle transformation back into her human-like form, Dracy allowed Alex and his companions to dismount, their eyes fixed on the tranquil waters before them.

Leading the group to the edge of the lake, Alex took a deep breath, steeling himself for the task ahead. Closing his eyes, he focused his mind, reaching out with his thoughts in an attempt to make contact with the Blue Turtle once more.

A few seconds passed, and then a familiar white mist began to swirl around them, enveloping Alex and his friends in its ethereal embrace. When the mist finally dissipated, they found themselves standing in the presence of the legendary Blue Turtle once again, its ancient eyes regarding them with a sense of quiet wisdom.

For Luna, Eirys, Theron, and Dracy, it was a moment of awe and wonder, their expressions a mixture of disbelief and reverence as they beheld the majestic creature before them. Luna, in particular, was unable to contain her excitement, her eyes shining with unbridled enthusiasm as she took in the sight before her.

"Oh, my stars! It's really you! I've read so much about you in the ancient texts, but I never imagined I'd actually get to see you in person!" she exclaimed, her voice tinged with awe.

The Blue Turtle regarded Luna with a gentle smile, its ancient eyes crinkling at the corners. "Ah, young one, your enthusiasm is a joy to behold," it replied, its voice warm and soothing. "It is rare to encounter one with such a thirst for knowledge and a genuine appreciation for the wonders of the world."

Luna's excitement only seemed to grow as she continued to pepper the Blue Turtle with questions, her curiosity seemingly boundless. "How old are you? What's it like living beneath the waters of the lake? Do you have any favorite stories from your long life?" she asked, her words tumbling out in a rush.

The Blue Turtle chuckled softly at Luna's barrage of questions, its gaze softening as it regarded the young mage with fondness. "I am as old as time itself, my dear, and my life beneath the waters is one of tranquility and contemplation," it replied, its voice filled with a wistful feeling. "As for stories, well, I have many tales to tell, each more wondrous than the last. But perhaps that is a conversation for another time."

After Luna had finally calmed down and the initial excitement had worn off, the Blue Turtle turned its attention to Alex, its gaze piercing and wise. "I assume you didn't just come here because you missed me, Alex?" it asked, a hint of amusement in its voice.

Alex grinned in response, his eyes sparkling with humor. "As much as I enjoyed our conversations, I'm afraid I have more pressing matters on my mind this time," he replied, his tone light despite the gravity of their situation.

The Blue Turtle listened intently as Alex recounted his adventure so far, the details of his dream, the appearance of Lilith and Alteoth, their meeting with the Elders, and so on.

"Lilith... So, she's appeared once again," it murmured, its voice tinged with concern. "It's funny how time goes by when you're trapped without any communication with the outside world. I would have imagined she would've perished by now."

Alex immediately remembered the Turtle's words during their last encounter. "Don't tell me... The sorceress that you mentioned had you imprisoned... was Lilith?" he asked, putting the dots together. It would certainly make sense.

"Yes, but that's no more what's important," the Turtle replied. "It seems like you have a lot on your hands, Alex. Master Shoi speaks the truth about what is needed for the replacement ritual - but I'm afraid it won't turn out to be an easy feat finding a suitable vassal and one who can guide the ritual with their magic. It is a dangerous path you tread, young one, but one that may be necessary to protect our world from the darkness that threatens to engulf it. Alas if I were not bound here, I could help you with at least one of those roles."

"Really? I'd hate to have you carry the responsibility, but I'm afraid I'm out of any more ideas," Alex said, a hint of regret in his voice. "As it happens to be, however, the Crystal of Unsealing you mentioned last time I was here was broken into three shards and we have managed to find two of the three shards of the

Crystal of Unsealing. But, unfortunately, we have no idea where the third one is. If only we had all of them, we could move one step closer to our goal," he added.

"Well, in that case, I might be able to help you out after all. Can you show me those shards, Alex?" the Blue Turtle asked, seeming to have something in mind.

Eirys immediately unpacked her bag and produced the two shards in her possession - one that the crow had gifted her and the one that they received as a reward from Kline for helping the village in the Land of Lost Tales. As she held them up on the palm of her hand, the Blue Turtle used its magic on them. The two shards lit up and the Turtle closed its eyes, seeming as though meditating.

The room went silent for a few seconds before the Turtle once again opened its eyes and announced, "I see it, the last shard - it's in Lilith's possession."

Amazed at the feat that the Turtle had just pulled off, Alex asked, "Are you sure?"

"Unfortunately, yes. I can use magic to detect the locations of the fragments of a whole object," the Turtle said lowly as everyone understood the implication of this.

With that, they had finally found a lead to follow, but it still didn't change the fact that they would have to face up to Lilith and Alteoth.

"Can you also tell us the location of where Lilith and the last shard is?" Luna asked, figuring that it would be good information to have for the next part of their journey. Alex looked over in an approving manner, as if he was thinking of asking the same thing.

"In the depths of the Bestial Kingdom of Jelan lies the Andel forest. You'll find them there, although I cannot specify the location any further," it replied. "If you're going up against them, I suppose you have a plan in mind, Alex?" the turtle asked then.

Chapter 11

The Bestial Kingdom

Alex took a deep breath and loosened himself up a bit. They had finally dived into the most important talk of this visit - the reason why Alex decided to come here at this time. Looking into its ancient eyes, Alex took a moment to gather his thoughts before responding.

"Actually, I wanted to ask you something," he began, his voice steady despite the tumult of emotions swirling within him. "Have you heard of the ritual to change the host for the origin tree?"

The Turtle's eyes focused, giving Alex the impression that he already knew. It would make sense considering that it had been revered as such as a wise and intelligent being.

"To save both Alteoth's daughter and the Origin Tree, we'll need two beings with immense magical power — one to cast the spell and one to take the current host's place," Alex continued.

The Blue Turtle listened intently, its wise gaze fixed on Alex as he spoke. After a moment of contemplation, it replied, "If you can set me free, I can be the one to cast the spell. It might not seem so judging from my current state, but my magic is on par with the gods of this world themselves. You'll still have to find someone to take the host's place, however."

Alex's heart soared with hope at the Blue Turtle's offer of help. Here was a being of unparalleled power, willing to aid them in their quest to save their world from darkness. "Thank you," he breathed, overwhelmed with gratitude. "I'll certainly obtain the last shard of the Crystal and see to it that you're finally free."

“I'll certainly look forward to it then,” it said, responding with a smile. As parting advice, the Turtle then warned them, “Be careful when you set foot inside the forest, however, for it is teeming with monsters and nefarious beings. Take this charm with you; it will help you in your direst time.”

A locket embedded with a beautiful blue gemstone appeared and Alex accepted it with gratitude.

“Thank you, Turtle. Thanks to you, we have found yet another beacon of hope. I have no doubts that we'll certainly succeed in our mission. I have been blessed with really great partners who've always got my back."

"I'll send you back to the lake now," it responded as the white mist once again appeared, enveloping everyone. As a last quip, Alex heard the Turtle's voice as the mist dissipated, "And Alex, my name is Julian."

Alex couldn't help but let out a smile. Just then, Luna voiced the question that lingered in all of their minds. "What should we do next, Alex?"

Alex turned to face her, his expression determined. "First, we have to find Alteoth," he replied, his voice resolute. "We're going straight to Bestial Kingdom of Jelan."

"But what about finding a replacement for the Origin Tree's host?" Luna asked, trying to make sense of what Alex had been thinking.

"About that, I've got something in mind. It might or might not work, but if it does, we'll save ourselves a lot of trouble," he replied, his mind already working out the details of his plan.

Luna seemed a bit unconvinced, but she decided to let it go for now. She trusted Alex and she knew that whatever he came up with was probably the most likely path to their success.

"If we're going into the Bestial Kingdom, we'll first need to get a permit. Flying straight in would only get us in trouble. They have pretty strict rules about these things," Eirys informed them as the only one who had been there before.

"Well, that changes things then," Alex replied, almost disappointed. "Where do we get a permit?" he then proceeded to ask.

"We'll have to get them from the Embassy in the Capital. They're honestly a bit difficult to work with, but we have good reason to be visiting. Maybe it won't be such a difficult task this time," Eirys replied, her face showing a clear expression of exhaustion recounting the last time she had to get one. Her work with medicine and magic often required her to travel to the deepest corners of the world of Echoes.

"In that case, let me check with the Elders once. Perhaps they can help us with that. As you can guess, they hold quite the influence," Luna suggested. With a swift motion of her hands, she produced her magic, creating a connection to Master Shoi.

"There's no need to worry. I'll have it taken care of. But you'll still have to come back to the Capital to receive the permits in person. I'll have them ready by the time you reach," said

Master Shoi promisingly once Luna explained the whole predicament to him.

And so, once again Alex and the others began their aerial adventure towards the Capital on Dracy's back.

Back at the Capital, the group wasted no time in making their way straight to the Embassy, where Master Shoi awaited them. On their arrival, he promptly gestured to someone who immediately brought them the permits.

"Take the permits and stay safe on your journey ahead. The fate of the world resides on your hands," Master Shoi encouraged Alex and the others.

"Thank you, Master Shoi. Your assistance has saved us a lot of time. We'll be on our way now," Luna replied.

Walking through the city streets, Alex had started to feel a bit anxious. He knew that the day he would have to confront Alteoth was drawing closer. But if his plan worked, there was a chance that that fight could be avoided. And for his sake and the others', he hoped his plans would bear fruit. Suddenly, breaking his line of thought, Alex heard Eirys' voice.

"Ughhh! I'm so hungry! When was the last time we ate, Luna? I feel like it was ages ago," she complained. And she had a point. Between flying and fighting bad guys, they had almost overlooked nutrition.

"In that case, let's go to my uncle's place. It's right in front of the market and I'll even get us a discount! I promised Alex I'd treat him some dumplings the next time we were in the Capital!" Dracy's enthusiasm suddenly skyrocketed.

Leading the group through the busy streets, she found her way to the marketplace. In front of them stood a rusty looking, but interestingly quite busy place with the board hanging above, "Drago's Restaurant". Together, they made their way in and sat down at the only empty table towards the back. The scent of spices and cooking wafted through the air, tantalizing their senses and making their mouths water.

Uncle Drogo took all of their orders and brought out some delicious looking meals. As they dug in, Dracy asked Alex what he thought about the dumplings. But Alex, with his mouth stuffed full, couldn't even answer her question. Instead, Dracy got her answer when Alex couldn't resist ordering a second serving, savoring every mouthful as if it were his last.

"I'll let you take this one, Dracy. Those were the best dumplings I've ever had!" he said, once he was done finishing every last one of them.

After a fulfilling meal, they bid farewell to Uncle Drago and set off towards the Bestial Kingdom. Dracy transformed into her dragon form once more, carrying them on her back as they soared through the sky towards their destination. Once the towering gates of the kingdom became visible, they decided to continue closing in on foot.

The guards at the gate verified their permits with a nod of approval, allowing them entry into the kingdom. The streets were bustling with activity, filled with merchants hawking their wares and travelers bustling about their business. The first thing Alex noticed was that there were all kinds of animals living together in this kingdom. There were cats and dogs as shopkeepers, lions and tigers working as guards, and all kinds of birds and animals living their daily lives together.

"I can understand. That's how I felt the first time I came here as well," Eirys said, almost in a taunting voice as she studied the expression on Alex's face. "I think the first thing we should do here is buy a map of the kingdom," she continued. Her experience being here previously was already proving useful.

Alex agreed with her suggestion and the group made their way to the marketplace. Stalls lined the streets, each one offering a variety of goods and wares, from exotic spices to finely crafted jewelry. After some searching, they managed to find a vendor selling maps of the kingdom. With the map in hand, they studied it carefully, tracing their route to the Andel Forest. Once they had their bearings, they set off once again on Dracy's back, soaring through the sky.

As they flew over the vast expanse of the kingdom, the landscape below shifted and changed, each new sight showing the various corners of the kingdom. But as they approached the Andel Forest, Dracy began to sense that something was amiss.

"We should be nearing the forest by now, but I can't seem to get a clear sense of direction," Dracy explained, her brow furrowed in concentration.

Alex felt a sense of unease creeping over him. It was strange indeed that they couldn't seem to find their way, he thought, even with the help of the map and Dracy's keen senses.

"Perhaps we're going in circles without realizing it," Theron mused, trying to figure out the possibilities. "Dracy, can you try following the direction of the sun? Maybe that will help us get back on track."

Dracy nodded, adjusting their course to follow the path of the sun. But even then, they seemed to be no closer to their destination.

"It's as if the forest itself is playing tricks on us," Luna remarked, her voice filled with wonder and apprehension.

Eirys nodded in agreement, her expression serious. "It's possible that the forest is enchanted, or that someone is casting a spell to keep us away. If that's the case, then it would seem that the Blue Turtle was right about their location."

Alex's mind raced as he considered their options. They were lost, stranded in the sky above a mysterious forest with no way of knowing which way to go.

"We need to do something to break through this enchantment," Eirys said, turning to Alex with a look of determination. "Do you have any ideas?"

Alex racked his brain, searching for a solution to their predicament. Then, suddenly, inspiration struck.

"I think I might have an idea," he said slowly, his eyes alight with determination. "But we'll have to see if that works."

He remembered something from his old stories about the Dreamseekers. While they were creatures who used illusions and hallucinations to lure in prey, they were also quite adept at countering illusory magic. With an incantation and a gesture, Alex once again used his summoning magic to call forth a Dreamseeker and tried using its magic to dispel the enchantment.

“Damn it!” Alex expressed his frustration as he soon found out that the enchantment was far too powerful to be undone by a single Dreamseeker. “There’s no doubt that this was cast by a powerful mage - either Lilith or Alteoth. It would take me summoning an entire army of Dreamseekers to dispel the enchantment, but unfortunately, I just don’t have enough magic in me for that,” he announced, dejectedly.

“Don’t worry, Alex! If that’s the problem, I know a spell we can use to combine our magic. With that, we can make up for the magic we need through our teamwork!" Luna spoke excitedly. She always wanted to use that spell, but in situations that actually mattered, it was always impractical because it took time to set up the spell. She figured now was the moment she would finally get to use it.

But Theron immediately put Luna's excitement to rest. "Don't be too hasty, Luna," he warned her. "Don't forget we are still in air. If we try summoning an army of Dreamseekers, even Dracy won't be able to carry us all. I'm sure there's a smarter way to do this."

"Oh? And what 'smarter' way have you thought of, Theron? Please do tell us," Luna replied, her voice almost spiteful for not being able to use the Spell of Consolidation.

"Dreamcatchers are quite good at navigating illusions, right? Why don't we just let this one try to find the source of the magic? All we need to do then is follow it through the enchanted forest," Theron suggested.

Luna stood dumbstruck for a second. Theron's idea actually made sense and it was far more efficient than what she and Alex thought of. They didn't necessarily have to dispel the enchantment; they only needed to find their way in.

And so, with its keen senses and natural resistance against illusory magic, the Dreamseeker led the group through the forest of Andel until they arrived right in front of a huge castle that stood quite out of place with the rest of the landscape of the forest.

"There's no doubt," said Luna as they stood at the entrance. "I can feel immense magic radiating from this castle. This must where Lilith and Alteoth are."

Chapter 12

Into the Enemy Lines

The group stood before the towering gates of the castle, their hearts pounding with anticipation. They had come this far, driven by a sense of purpose and the hope of saving Alteoth's daughter and the world from darkness. As they prepared themselves for the battle ahead, the gates slowly creaked open, revealing the dimly lit interior of the castle beyond.

"I think we've been invited in," Alex remarked, his voice tinged with uncertainty. "Well, in that case, let's take up on their offer. But be careful at all times," Theron advised, his eyes scanning their surroundings for any signs of danger.

With cautious steps, they entered the castle, the echoes of their footsteps reverberating through the empty halls. The air was heavy with the scent of age and decay, and the walls seemed to whisper secrets of times long past. As they navigated the labyrinthine passages, they stumbled upon forgotten ruins and hidden chambers, each one holding its own mystery and danger.

Finally, after what felt like hours of wandering, they found themselves standing in the central hall of the castle. At the far end of the hall, seated upon a throne-like chair, was Alteoth, his imposing figure bathed in shadows. Standing beside him was Lilith, her presence radiating an aura of malevolence.

Alex's heart skipped a beat as he recognized Alteoth from his dream, the memory of their encounter still fresh in his mind. He quickly relayed this information to the others, who tensed at the sight of their enemy.

"Why did you allow us in so easily?" Alex asked, his voice betraying his confusion. "I was expecting to fight more monsters on the way."

"This is our first time meeting, Alex," Alteoth replied, his voice calm and measured. "I've heard about you and your group from Lilith. I believe she speaks the truth about your strength, which means that sending low-level monsters to fight you would only get them killed for nothing. Moreover, it doesn't feel right if we fight and kill each other the very first day we meet, right? I believe we need to know each other to understand who we're fighting against."

"For someone trying to destroy the world, you're quite courteous," Alex remarked, his tone tinged with skepticism.

"From my perspective, I'm only trying to save my daughter," Alteoth explained, his voice tinged with sorrow. "But I wouldn't expect you to understand that. For now, I don't intend to fight you, but if you have anything to say, I'm willing to hear."

Alex took a deep breath, steeling himself for what was to come. "We know about your daughter," he began, his voice steady despite the tumult of emotions swirling within him. "And we want to help you save her."

Alteoth's eyes widened in surprise, clearly taken aback by Alex's unexpected offer of assistance. "What do you mean?" he asked, his voice tinged with uncertainty.

Alex explained the dream that he had been having and their plan to help Alteoth save his daughter through the ritual that Master Shoi told them about. He spoke of their encounter with the Blue Turtle and its offer of help, but emphasized that they needed Alteoth to take his daughter's place as the host.

For a moment, Alteoth was silent, lost in thought as he weighed his options. Then, with a determined nod, he spoke. "I will help you save my daughter," he declared, his voice resolute. "But I will need to know the exact conditions of the ritual and how you plan to proceed."

Alex explained their plan in detail, outlining the steps they would need to take to save Elara and restore balance to the world. As he spoke, he could see the tension in Alteoth's shoulders ease slightly, replaced by a sense of hope and determination.

Once he had heard everything, Alteoth fell silent, his gaze fixed on the ground as he pondered their next move. Then, suddenly, without warning, Lilith let out a blood-curdling scream, her eyes blazing with fury as she drove a sword with black flames into Alteoth's chest.

"Alteoth!" Alex cried out, his heart pounding in his chest as he watched in horror. But it was too late - the damage had been done.

Alteoth's flesh began to blacken and warp, his body contorting in agony as the corruption spread through his veins. Alex and the others could only watch helplessly as he was consumed by darkness, eventually losing conscious resemblance of the man he was.

Slowly recovering from the shock, Alex was about to question his obvious curiosity when Lilith's laughter echoed through the hall, her eyes alight with madness as she regarded Alteoth's corrupted body with a twisted smile. "All these years, I loved you," she said, her voice dripping with venom. "But you never loved me in return. And now, you will be mine, whether you like it or not."

A chill ran down Alex's spine as he realized the extent of Lilith's madness. The revelation of her twisted love for Alteoth sent a shiver through the room. It was becoming clear that she had been planning this all along, manipulating events to suit her own twisted desires.

"Why would you do such a thing?" Alex demanded, his voice trembling with disbelief. "How could you betray someone you claim to love?"

Lilith's laughter filled the air, a cruel sound that sent shivers down Alex's spine. "A little mortal like you could perhaps never understand, but for us, love is power. And I will not be denied what should have been mine. I loved him since we were kids - since before I can even remember right now."

She seems distant for a moment, but then, with an awfully vengeful look on her face, decided to amuse Alex's question before wiping them off as her next targets. As she looked right at the corrupting body of Alteoth, Lilith reminisced, "Alteoth was always taking care of me and helping me out. He was kind, and I loved him for that. But he never fell in love with me.

Instead, he loved Elana and had a child with her. Since Elana died, I thought Alteoth would soon turn to me. And yet, all he did was spend years trying to save his daughter. He just wouldn't give up over that weakling and her child! "

As Lilith's emotions spill forth, her voice trembles with a mixture of rage and sorrow, her words dripping with venomous spite. Each syllable is infused with the pain of unrequited love and the seething hatred born from betrayal. Her hands clench into fists at her sides, nails digging into her palms as she struggles to contain the tempest raging within her.

Yet, despite the turmoil writhing beneath the surface, there is a cold, calculated edge to her demeanor, a steely resolve that belies the storm of emotions raging within. Behind the facade of composure, Lilith's heart beats with a frenzied rhythm, consumed by the flames of vengeance burning bright within her soul.

"But why go so far to help him then? It seems like you already had planned to use that sword on him. Why didn't you do it sooner?" Luna demanded, even though she could barely stand and think straight from the intense turn of events.

"I offered him my help, but only I knew that I was planning to slowly kill Elara with those corruptions," she continued, her words laced with malice. "Sure, I already had planned to use the sword of corruption to make Alteoth mine, but that would've been much later - once I had completely gotten rid of Elana's child. I wanted to see the look on his face before I made him mine! But all of my plans were foiled since you and your companions barged into our castle. I can't forgive you for that, can I?"

With her confessions laid bare, Lilith makes it clear that an ugly battle was now unavoidable.

Chapter 13

The Origin Tree

Alex and the others clenched their fists tightly in anticipation of Lilith's next move. With a roar, she launched beams of dark energy towards them one after another. Luna was ready with her defence magic and created a shield around her teammates. Breaking through Lilith's first wave of attack, Alex and Theron understood that they just couldn't sit there and do nothing while Lilith was hell-bent on destroying them. The two quickly adjusted their positioning and took the vanguard like they had been doing so far.

The air crackled with tension as Alex and his companions squared off against Lilith, their eyes locked in a deadly dance of determination and defiance. The grand hall echoed with the hum of magic, each pulse of power sending ripples through the very fabric of reality.

Lilith stood at the center of the room, her form wreathed in swirling shadows and tendrils of dark energy. Her eyes blazed with an unholy light, the twisted remnants of her love for Alteoth fueling her every movement. Beside her, the corrupted form of Alteoth loomed like a specter of doom, his once noble features twisted into a grotesque mockery of his former self.

Alex gritted his teeth, his hands clenched into fists at his sides as he prepared to face his greatest adversary yet. He could feel the weight of the moment pressing down upon him, the fate of the world hanging in the balance. With a silent nod to his companions, he stepped forward, his gaze never wavering from Lilith's dark form.

The battle erupted in a flurry of spells and incantations, the air alive with the crackle of magic and the clash of steel. Luna conjured shields of shimmering energy to deflect Lilith's dark tendrils, while Eirys unleashed torrents of flame to drive back the encroaching darkness. Theron moved with the speed and grace of a seasoned warrior, his blade slicing through the shadows with deadly precision.

But despite their valiant efforts, Lilith proved to be a formidable foe, her magic weaving through their defenses with effortless grace. With a flick of her wrist, she sent waves of dark energy crashing against their shields, threatening to overwhelm them with sheer force. And as the battle raged on, the corrupted form of Alteoth joined the fray, his powers adding an even greater threat to their already dire situation.

Dracy roared with fury, her draconic form unleashing torrents of flame to drive back their assailants. But even her formidable strength was no match for the combined might of Lilith and the corrupted Alteoth. With each passing moment, the odds seemed to shift further in their enemy's favor, their strength waning against the relentless onslaught.

Desperation clawed at Alex's heart as he struggled to find a way to turn the tide of battle. He knew that they couldn't hope to defeat Lilith and Alteoth in their current state, not with their powers augmented by the corruption that now consumed them. But as he glanced around at his companions, a flicker of determination ignited within him.

"Change of plans," he shouted over the din of battle, his voice ringing with resolve. "We need to focus our efforts on separating Lilith from Alteoth. That's our only chance of winning this."

With renewed determination, Alex and his companions rallied together, their magic intertwining in a symphony of light and shadow. Luna channeled her energy into a powerful barrier, while Eirys unleashed torrents of flame to drive back their enemies. Theron moved with lightning speed, his blade flashing as he danced through the chaos.

But even as they fought with all their might, Lilith and the corrupted Alteoth seemed to anticipate their every move, their attacks growing more relentless with each passing moment. It was as if they were playing a game of chess, each move calculated to keep them on the defensive.

As the battle raged on, Alex and his group found themselves locked in a desperate struggle against the corrupt form of Alteoth. But with each passing moment, the tide of battle seemed to shift in their favor, their spells and incredible teamwork eventually wearing out Lilith's defenses. Luna's magic was working quite effectively against Alteoth as well. Due to the special characteristic of her magic, little by little, it seemed like Alteoth's corruption was receding until eventually at one point, he stopped attacking and instead seemed to be regaining his consciousness.

The grand hall trembled with the intensity of the battle as Alex and his companions faced off against Lilith and Alteoth's corrupted form, their magic intertwining in a struggle for victory. But just as the tide began to turn in their favor, Lilith's desperate declaration sent a chill down their spines.

"I've had enough with all of you!" she cried in pure rage-filled madness. "I'm going to uproot the Origin Tree and end all of this once and for all!"

Declaring her intention, Lilith promptly retreats from the fight and sets off towards the Origin Tree, leaving Alex and the others to fight against Alteoth alone. But knowing that Luna's light magic was working against Alteoth's corruption, they knew that they would eventually be able to subdue Alteoth. The problem was that even knowing that this was Lilith's way of buying time, they still had no choice but to first deal with Alteoth.

Luna screamed in frustration, "That witch! She's never up to any good!"

Alteoth's incoming attack was a reminder to them that they were still in the middle of an engagement. With Theron's command, everyone quickly returned to formation while him and Alex closed in on Alteoth. In the meantime, Luna resorted to a barrage of attacks directed at Alteoth. With the two in the front keeping him engaged and distracted, Luna was able to get quite a few hits in.

Eventually, their tactics worked. Alteoth had once again regained consciousness.

“I’m sorry... for what Lilith did,” he said as his memories returned. “I never meant for any of this to happen. Lilith... she's always been so... lost. It’s my fault.”

Alex placed a reassuring hand on Alteoth's shoulder, his gaze filled with sympathy. "It's not your fault," he said softly. "We'll find a way to stop her, I promise."

Alteoth nodded, a determined look crossing his face. "We have to act fast. Lilith will stop at nothing to achieve her goals. Unfortunately, at our current condition, we might barely be able to put up a fight against her. So, instead of defeating her, we have to try sealing her away for good. That’s the best chance we have at saving my daughter."

"Sealing her instead of trying to defeat her... That might just work," Alex mused, his mind racing with possibilities. "Luna, do you really know a sealing spell?"

Luna nodded, her eyes alight with excitement. "Yes, I do. But it's not going to be easy. The spell requires a tremendous amount of magic power, and it'll take time to set up. We'll need all the help we can get."

Alteoth nodded solemnly. "Between your magic and mine, I believe we can handle the spellcasting," he said. "However, considering my current state, unfortunately, we may not have enough magic energy."

"You're right," Luna agreed. "Which is why," she exclaimed as her eyes lit up with excitement," I think this is the perfect time to test out the Spell of Consolidation!"

"It seems like you really want to use that spell, Luna," Alex replied, with a sigh.

"Well, of course! It's my own speciality spell. I created it," she explained an expression of pride washed over her face.

"Fine. We'll use it," Alex responded as he understood why Luna was so eager to show the spell off. "But how exactly does it work?" he asked.

"Oh, you won't have to do much. I'll simply cast a spell and transfer some magic energy from all of you to me," Luna explained, a mischievous smile. "Don't worry," she reassured them, "I'll leave enough for you guys to be able to fight."

"Leave me with enough energy to make it back to the Capital for some dumplings, and we're all good!" Dracy said in a joking manner, uplifting some unnecessary tension before a final fight against Lilith.

“Leaving Luna and Alteoth to handle the sealing magic, Alex and I will be in the frontline as usual and try to buy as much time as we can,” Theron chimed in his idea from the side.

Eirys and Dracy exchanged a knowing glance. "We'll focus on ranged attacks and healing," Eirys said, her voice steady. "We'll do whatever it takes to support you."

With their plan set, the group began to prepare in earnest. Just then, Alteoth's expression grew grave, a shadow passing over his features. "I hope it's not too late," he murmured, his voice heavy with concern. "If Lilith has reached the Origin Tree..."

Luna's eyes widened in realization. "There’s no need for worry then," she said, her voice steady, "we're in luck. I can teleport us there directly."

Dracy's expression soured at the mention of teleportation, her features contorting into a grimace. "Teleporting? I wanted to fly us there," she grumbled, her wings twitching with frustration.

Eirys raised an eyebrow, a thoughtful expression crossing her features. "In that case," she said slowly, "I suggest a slight change of plans."

With a flick of her wrist, Eirys produced three shimmering shards of the Crystal of Unsealing, each one pulsing with energy on the top of her palm. The group stared in astonishment, their minds racing with possibilities.

"I swept the last piece off of Lilith during our battle," Eirys explained, her voice steady. "I think it would save us a lot of time if Dracy and I went separately to undo the Blue Turtle's seal. We may not have enough time otherwise," she said, considering the fact that Alteoth's corruption had already weakened him a lot.

Alex grinned, his eyes shining with excitement. "I like the sound of that," he declared. "We'll split into two teams: one to chase after Lilith, and one to free the Blue Turtle."

Luna's brow furrowed with concern. "I can understand Dracy doesn't like teleportation, but Eirys is our only healer. What if we need her while fighting Lilith?" she asked, her voice tinged with uncertainty.

Alteoth reassured Luna in his calm, deep voice, his eyes filled with a calm confidence.

“Having fought against you all, I can tell that you’re strong. But just in case, I have something for both Alex and Theron,” he said as he retrieved two small vials from his cloak, their contents shimmering like an extremely rare potion.

"These will help you resist almost all attacks for at least a good few minutes," he explained, handing the vial to Theron and Alex. "With these Potion of Invulnerability, we should have more than enough, considering that this time we’re not trying to defeat her.”

Theron nodded, his fingers closing around the vial with gratitude. "This will certainly help us if things get too difficult," he noted.

Further reassuring Luna, Alteoth said, "Moreover, even in my current state, I can still put up a fight against Lilith. And with our new plan in place, I believe we stand a fighting chance."

Alex nodded, his resolve hardening with each passing moment. "With Lilith somewhat weakened, and a solid plan in place, I'm feeling much more confident about our chances," he declared, his voice ringing with determination.

Luna hesitated for a moment, her eyes flickering with uncertainty. But as she looked around at her companions, she saw the fire of determination burning bright in their eyes. With a silent nod, she squared her shoulders, her resolve hardening with each passing moment.

"Let's do this," she said, her voice steady. "For Echoes, and for all those who call it home."

And with that, the group split into two teams, each one ready to face whatever challenges lay ahead. Eirys and Dracy took the castle's exit and flew from there while Luna prepared her teleportation spell. Once she was done, the four of them, including Luna, Alteoth, Alex, and Theron, walked through the portal.

Immediately after walking in through the portal, Alex noted the vast, clear valley with beautiful lush grass all over the landscape. The Origin Tree stood majestically; its towering branches stretched towards the sky. As they drew closer, however, they could notice that something was terribly wrong.

The once vibrant leaves of the tree now drooped with despair, their colors faded and dull. Magic energy seemed to be oozing out of the tree as the very essence of the tree seemed to pulse with a faint, dying light, as if struggling to hold on against an unseen force.

Luna gasped in horror at the sight before her. "The Origin Tree," she whispered, her voice trembling with emotion. "It's dying."

Alteoth's expression darkened as he surveyed the scene before him. "Lilith," he growled, his voice filled with barely contained rage. "She's uprooted the tree, and now it's dying. We have to stop her before it's too late."

The dark sorceress stood before the uprooted tree; her form wreathed in shadows as she channeled her dark magic into the very heart of the ancient tree. Her eyes blazed with an unholy light, the twisted remnants of her love for Alteoth fueling her every movement.

“I see that you have joined their side as well, Alteoth. But it’s all good!” Lilith shouted as she laughed in a mad rage, gazing right at Alteoth. “Because today I’m going to end it all! You, me, and everyone else.”

“You know that’s not what you want, Lilith. Please stop this,” Alteoth tried requesting one last time before the fight continued between them.

Lilith, however, was in no mood for any kind of conversation. It seemed like she was as determined to destroy this world, and many others with it, as was Luna in saving it.

“You can try, Lilith, but we’re going to stop you anyway,” Luna said to her, almost in a promising way. “We’re going to save the world and bring peace back.”

”Big words coming from someone who couldn’t stop me back then from creating the abyss. I heard they even gave it a grand name – the Incident of the Lost Tales. I wonder if it still haunts you that you lost to me in that fight and ended up being responsible for the deaths of so many,” Lilith replied to Luna’s provocation, causing Luna to seethe in rage and vengeance.

Without one more word, Luna extended her arms, casting a spell, and launching it directly at Lilith. Lilith instantly deflected it with one hand and returned one of her own spells, causing Alex and the others to instantly assume their battle formation.

With a roar of fury, Alex and his companions charged forward, their weapons raised high as they prepared to face their greatest challenge yet. But as they drew closer, they could feel the power of the corrupted tree radiating outwards, threatening to overwhelm them with its sheer force.

With a surge of determination, they unleashed a barrage of attacks against Lilith, their magic intertwining in a symphony of light and shadow. But despite their valiant efforts, Lilith's dark magic proved to be a formidable foe, her power weaving through their defenses with effortless grace.

Chapter 14

The Final Confrontation

The battlefield was a chaotic whirlwind, with the uprooted Origin Tree standing as a dying testament to the gravity of the conflict. Alex and Theron stood side by side, their weapons gleaming under the faint light filtering through the thick canopy of twisted branches. Luna and Alteoth positioned themselves behind the warriors, their hands already weaving the intricate patterns of the sealing magic.

Lilith stood before them, her eyes burning with a fierce, unyielding malice. Her lips curled into a sardonic smile as she watched the preparations, her dark aura pulsating with sinister energy.

"You really think you can seal me away?" Lilith's voice dripped with contempt. "Pathetic."

"Let's see how you handle this," Theron growled, charging forward with Alex right behind him.

Lilith's laughter echoed through the clearing as she raised her hands, summoning a massive black dragon from the shadows. The creature was a nightmarish vision, with scales that absorbed the light and seemed to suck the very life from the air around it. Its eyes glowed a malevolent red, and each breath it took emitted a toxic fog that withered the plants at its feet. The dragon's wings were vast, stretching out like blackened sails, and when it unfurled them, the wind howled with a mournful wail. Its roar, when it came, was a sound of pure dread, shaking the very earth and rattling the bones of those who heard it.

Alex's eyes widened in shock and determination. "That's... a black dragon! Stay on your guard!" he shouted to the others, the gravity of the situation hitting him hard.

Theron tightened his grip on his sword, his knuckles whitening. "We take down Lilith, and the dragon follows," he said, trying to reassure himself as much as the others.

The beast lunged towards Luna and Alteoth, disrupting their spellcasting with a single, mighty swipe of its clawed hand. The force of the blow sent them sprawling, their concentration shattered.

"Focus, Alteoth!" Luna shouted over the chaos, her voice steady despite the mounting pressure.

"We don't have much time!" Alteoth responded, his hands trembling slightly as he tried to maintain his concentration.

Seeing the dragon's attack, Alex and Theron redoubled their efforts, aiming to distract Lilith. The ground quaked beneath their feet as they clashed with her, their weapons ringing out against her dark energy shield. Lilith moved with a deadly grace, her magic creating barriers and blasts that countered their every move. The air around her crackled with malevolent energy, distorting the space and making it hard for Alex and Theron to land a hit.

Theron feinted to the left, then spun and aimed a low slash at Lilith's legs, hoping to throw her off balance. She anticipated the move, leaping into the air with an almost supernatural agility. Alex seized the moment to strike, aiming a powerful overhead blow at her exposed back. Lilith twisted in mid-air, her dark blade materializing just in time to parry his attack.

"You're resilient," Lilith sneered, parrying Theron's sword strike with ease. "But can you handle this?"

With a swift motion, Lilith knocked Theron back and spun to face Alex, who dodged her initial strike and countered with a quick slash aimed at her midsection. She twisted away, her movements fluid and almost graceful despite the raw power behind them. She retaliated with a burst of dark energy, forcing Alex to roll out of the way to avoid being hit.

"Luna, we need to hurry!" Alex shouted, barely avoiding another of Lilith's lethal strikes. His breath came in ragged gasps as he tried to maintain his focus amidst the chaos.

Alex and Theron were barely holding up against Lilith. Every clash with her felt like a fight against a force of nature. Their muscles screamed in protest, and their breaths came in short, desperate gasps. The once vibrant forest was now a battlefield of dying magic, the energy seeping from the Origin Tree creating an oppressive atmosphere. Its branches, once teeming with life, hung limp and lifeless, the brilliant green leaves turning to ash and falling to the ground in a slow, mournful rain.

"We're running out of time," Alex muttered, his eyes flicking to the tree. "If we don't stop her soon, Elara and the entire realm will be lost."

Theron gritted his teeth, deflecting another of Lilith's attacks. "We can't afford to think about failure. We have to give Luna and Alteoth the time they need."

The urgency in Luna's voice was palpable as she and Alteoth tried to refocus their efforts. "Alteoth, we mustn't fail. The tree is dying."

Alteoth nodded, his resolve hardening as he focused on completing the spell. His mind raced, filled with images of Elara and the countless lives depending on their success. His heart ached with the weight of responsibility, and he could feel his own magic faltering under the pressure.

"I won't let you down, Elara," Alteoth whispered to himself, renewing his determination.

The black dragon roared again, its fiery breath scorching the ground near Luna and Alteoth, forcing them to dodge and interrupting their spell once more. Each attack from the dragon sent shockwaves through the ground, making it difficult for them to find stable footing.

"Keep that beast away from them!" Alex shouted to Theron, who nodded and moved to engage the dragon, trying to draw its attention.

Theron swung his sword in wide arcs, aiming to distract the dragon and give Luna and Alteoth a chance to cast their spell. The dragon, however, was relentless, its claws slicing through the air with deadly precision. Each swing of Theron's sword met with the dragon's impenetrable scales, barely leaving a scratch.

"Luna, we need more time!" Alteoth cried, his voice strained with the effort of maintaining his focus amidst the chaos.

"I'm trying, but that thing won't let up!" Luna responded, her eyes darting between the dragon and the spell they were attempting to cast.

As the battle raged on, the Origin Tree continued to wither, its magical energy seeping away like water from a cracked vessel. The ground around it was littered with fallen leaves, their once vibrant hues now dull and lifeless. The tree's bark, once strong and sturdy, was now brittle and flaking away, revealing the raw, vulnerable core beneath.

"We're losing it," Alex muttered, his eyes fixed on the tree. "We can't hold out much longer."

Lilith, sensing their desperation, pressed her advantage. "Your efforts are futile," she taunted, her voice echoing through the clearing. "This realm will fall, and you along with it."

"Not if we can help it," Alex shot back, his resolve hardening. He lunged at Lilith with renewed determination, his sword clashing against her dark energy shield.

Theron, meanwhile, was engaged in a deadly dance with the black dragon. Every swing of his sword was met with a counterattack from the beast, its claws and teeth coming perilously close to ending his life. Sweat poured down his face as he pushed himself to his limits, each moment a desperate struggle to survive.

In a brief moment of respite, Theron glanced over at Luna and Alteoth, who were now chanting in unison, their voices rising above the din of battle. The air around them shimmered with magical energy, the spell slowly taking shape. But the dragon was relentless, and it was clear that they needed more time.

"Luna, Alteoth, keep going!" Alex shouted, his voice carrying a note of desperation. "We'll hold them off!"

Lilith's eyes narrowed as she watched the spell forming. "I won't let you seal me away!" she screamed, unleashing a wave of dark magic that sent Alex and Theron reeling.

Alex hit the ground hard, the impact knocking the wind out of him. He struggled to his feet, his vision swimming as he tried to focus. "Theron... we have to... keep fighting..."

Theron, equally battered, nodded. "We can't let her win."

As they struggled to their feet, the air around them seemed to hum with an ominous energy. Lilith stood tall, her dark aura flaring with renewed intensity. "You will all fall before me," she declared, her voice dripping with malice.

But even as she spoke, there was a flicker of movement in the sky. A voice echoed through the air, strong and clear. "Hold on!"

Dracy, the majestic dragon, descended from the heavens, ramming into Lilith's dragon with incredible force. Lilith was knocked off balance, struggling to regain control as Dracy's powerful presence dominated the airspace.

"Eirys!" Alex exclaimed as he saw her and the blue turtle arriving on the scene. "You're just in time!"

While Lilith was recovering from her fall, Eirys took this chance to get to work. She approached Alex and Theron, who had taken quite some damage by now. Although their experience fighting against Lilith and her minions up until now had allowed them to fight without yet sustaining any grave injuries, they weren't completely unharmed either. Using her healing spells, she immediately started channeling her healing magic on both of them.

"We saw what was happening," Eirys explained as she healed them, dismounting the blue turtle. "Dracy dropped us off just before the fight started."

Dracy engaged the black dragon in a fierce aerial battle, giving Luna and Alteoth the time they needed to refocus on their spell. The blue turtle watched the unfolding battle solemnly, aware of the irony in Lilith's impending fate.

With Dracy keeping the black dragon occupied, Alex and Theron turned their attention back to Lilith, who had landed unsteadily on the ground. Her dark energy flared, but it was clear she was running out of strength.

"You can't win," Alex said, his voice firm. "This ends now."

Lilith's eyes blazed with defiance, but there was a flicker of fear. "I won't go down without a fight."

"Then we'll give you one," Theron replied, charging at her with renewed vigor.

The two warriors attacked in unison, their strikes precise and unrelenting. Lilith parried and countered, but each movement grew more labored, her energy waning with each passing second.

In the background, Luna and Alteoth's chanting grew louder, the air crackling with magical energy. The sealing spell was nearly complete.

Lilith, now cornered and desperate, let out a cry of fury, summoning the last of her strength to unleash a powerful wave of dark magic. Alex and Theron braced themselves, using their combined strength to withstand the onslaught.

"It's over, Lilith!" Alex shouted, pushing forward against the dark energy. "You can't escape this time!"

With a final, synchronized strike, Alex and Theron broke through her defenses, sending her sprawling to the ground. At that moment, Luna and Alteoth released the sealing spell, a brilliant light enveloping Lilith.

"No! This can't be!" Lilith screamed, struggling against the magical bonds.

The energy formed around her, binding her movements and pulling her towards a separate dimension. Her screams echoed through the battlefield as the spell took hold, sealing her away for eternity.

The blue turtle observed solemnly, its eyes reflecting the weight of the moment. "After all those years of keeping me trapped, it's poetic justice that Lilith meets the same fate."

As the light faded and silence settled over the battlefield, Alex, Theron, Luna, Alteoth, Eirys, Dracy, and the blue turtle stood together, their breaths heavy but victorious.

"It's finally over," Luna said softly, her voice filled with relief.

"Yes," Alex agreed, looking around at his friends. "But we couldn't have done it without each other."

Theron clapped a hand on Alex's shoulder. "We make a good team."

Alex smiled, feeling a deep sense of camaraderie. "That we do. Now, let's see what we can do to help the Origin Tree."

Together, they turned their attention to the dying tree, determined to restore the balance and heal the realm of Echoes. The battle had been won, but their journey was far from over.

The two warriors attacked in unison, their strikes precise and unrelenting. Lilith parried and countered, but each movement grew more labored, her energy waning with each passing second.

In the background, Luna and Alteoth's chanting grew louder, the air crackling with magical energy. The sealing spell was nearly complete.

Lilith, now cornered and desperate, let out a cry of fury, summoning the last of her strength to unleash a powerful wave of dark magic. Alex and Theron braced themselves, using their combined strength to withstand the onslaught.

"It's over, Lilith!" Alex shouted, pushing forward against the dark energy. "You can't escape this time!"

With a final, synchronized strike, Alex and Theron broke through her defenses, sending her sprawling to the ground. At that moment, Luna and Alteoth released the sealing spell, a brilliant light enveloping Lilith.

"No! This can't be!" Lilith screamed, struggling against the magical bonds.

The energy formed around her, binding her movements and pulling her towards a separate dimension. Her screams echoed through the battlefield as the spell took hold, sealing her away for eternity.

The blue turtle observed solemnly, its eyes reflecting the weight of the moment. "After all those years of keeping me trapped, it's poetic justice that Lilith meets the same fate."

As the light faded and silence settled over the battlefield, Alex, Theron, Luna, Alteoth, Eirys, Dracy, and the blue turtle stood together, their breaths heavy but victorious.

"It's finally over," Luna said softly, her voice filled with relief.

"Yes," Alex agreed, looking around at his friends. "But we couldn't have done it without each other."

Theron clapped a hand on Alex's shoulder. "We make a good team."

Alex smiled, feeling a deep sense of camaraderie. "That we do. Now, let's see what we can do to help the Origin Tree."

Together, they turned their attention to the dying tree, determined to restore the balance and heal the realm of Echoes. The battle had been won, but their journey was far from over.

Chapter 15

A New Adventure Begins

As the dust settled from their hard-fought battle, Alex approached Eirys with a mixture of relief and curiosity. "Did you have any trouble on your way here?" he asked, glancing at the blue turtle and Dracy.

Eirys shook her head, her face breaking into a smile. "It was as uneventful as could be, considering the circumstances," she replied. "We reached the lake without any issues. Dracy and I used the three shards to undo the sealing spell, and that's when we freed the legendary blue turtle."

The blue turtle, standing nearby, chuckled softly. "I must admit, I was a bit worried when Dracy told me she would fly me here. It was my first time riding a dragon," he confessed, his voice carrying a light, humorous tone.

Dracy snorted, her eyes twinkling with amusement. "You handled it well for a first-timer," she said, nudging the turtle gently with her nose.

The group shared a moment of laughter, the tension easing slightly. But the sense of impending crisis remained. They still had a crucial task to complete: the ritual to save the Origin Tree and, by extension, Elara.

Alteoth stepped forward, his expression serious. "I can hear Elara's voice trying to reach me," he said, his eyes filled with urgency. "She's saying we don't have much time."

Alteoth's declaration hung in the air, the weight of his words sinking in. He looked up, his gaze distant but determined. "Elara, I will save you," he vowed, his voice unwavering.

The blue turtle regarded Alteoth with a solemn expression. "Are you sure about this? Once you take her place, you won't see the world again."

Alteoth nodded, his eyes filled with resolve. "I'm sure. The corruption is taking over my body, and I don't have much time left anyway. I just want to save Elara and give her the chance at life she's been denied for all these years."

The gravity of Alteoth's decision weighed heavily on everyone, but there was no turning back. They moved to the base of the dying Origin Tree, preparing for the ritual.

The blue turtle took his position as the mediator, his ancient powers already stirring the air with a palpable sense of magic. "Everyone, get ready," he instructed, his voice calm and authoritative. "Alteoth, start pouring your energy into the root of the Origin Tree."

Alteoth closed his eyes, summoning his strength and focusing his energy. He placed his hands on the gnarled roots of the Origin Tree, feeling its pain and desperation. A soft glow began to emanate from his palms, spreading through the roots and into the heart of the tree.

The blue turtle began to chant in an ancient, melodic language, his voice resonating with the earth itself. The ground beneath them trembled slightly, responding to the turtle's call. The air around them shimmered, filled with the essence of magic.

Alteoth's energy flowed steadily into the tree, his life force intertwining with the dying roots. His face showed a mixture of pain and peace, as if he were pouring not just his power, but his very soul into the task. The Origin Tree responded, its branches quivering and leaves rustling as the magic took hold.

Luna, Alex, Theron, Eirys, and Dracy watched in awe as the ritual unfolded. Light swirled around Alteoth and the tree, creating a dazzling display of colours. The blue turtle's chanting grew louder, more intense, and the energy in the air thickened.

As the ritual reached its climax, Alteoth's body began to dissolve into particles of light. His form shimmered and faded, but his expression remained peaceful, a soft smile gracing his lips as he looked towards the sky. "Elara, live well," he whispered, his voice barely audible above the magical hum.

With a final surge of light, Alteoth's body dissipated completely, merging with the Origin Tree. The dying tree began to transform, its broken branches mending, its leaves turning a vibrant green once more. Where Alteoth had stood, a new Origin Tree emerged, its trunk strong and its foliage lush and full of life. This new tree radiated a serene, calming energy, a beacon of hope and renewal.

The new Origin Tree was a sight to behold. Its trunk was a rich, golden-brown, imbued with a gentle glow that seemed to pulse with life. The leaves were a deep emerald green, shimmering with an almost otherworldly light. Flowers of every colour bloomed along its branches, releasing a sweet, fragrant scent that filled the air. The tree's roots spread wide and deep, anchoring it firmly in the ground, and small, delicate vines wrapped around the trunk, their blossoms adding to the tree's beauty.

Where the broken Origin Tree had lain, now appeared a young girl. As she slowly opened her eyes, tears began to roll down her face. She looked around, her eyes wide with wonder and sorrow.

Alex and the others walked up to her, their hearts aching for the girl who had been through so much. Luna knelt beside her, wrapping her arms around the girl gently. "Why are you crying, Elara?" she asked softly.

Elara shrugged, her voice trembling. "I was just... wishing my father goodbye," she said, her tears flowing freely.

Seeing her pain, Alex and the others tried to console her, their hearts breaking at the sight of her grief. They spoke gentle words of comfort, offering their support and understanding.

Meanwhile, the blue turtle approached the new Origin Tree. He carefully broke off a small branch and, using his special magic, enchanted it. The branch transformed into a beautiful, ornate ring, glowing softly with a gentle light. He walked over to Elara, holding out the ring.

"This ring," the blue turtle explained, "will allow you to talk to your father's spirit within the Origin Tree, no matter where you are."

Elara's eyes lit up with joy as she took the ring, her tears turning to tears of happiness. She hugged the blue turtle tightly, her heart filled with gratitude. "Thank you," she whispered, her voice choked with emotion.

She then carefully put on the ring, her fingers trembling slightly as she slid it onto her hand. She closed her eyes and took a deep breath, focusing her thoughts. "Father, can you hear me?" she asked softly.

A warm, comforting voice responded in her mind. "Yes, Elara. I can hear you."

Tears welled up in her eyes once more, but this time they were tears of joy. "I'm so sorry you have to stay imprisoned within the Origin Tree for me," she said, her voice breaking.

Alteoth's spirit spoke with gentle reassurance. "Do not worry, my dear. I am quite happy that I can now look after the world like you had for all these years. Your sacrifice has not gone unnoticed."

Elara smiled through her tears, feeling a profound sense of peace wash over her. "Thank you, Father. I promise to live my life to the fullest, just as you wanted."

Once Elara had calmed down, Alteoth's voice turned to Alex. "Alex, I want my daughter to experience the world that she has held together for so long. Will you take her with you on your journey?"

Alex looked at Elara, a warm smile spreading across his face. "Elara, would you like to join us on our journey?" he asked.

Elara nodded enthusiastically, her eyes shining with excitement. "Yes, I would love that," she replied.

The group stood together, united by their shared experiences and the bonds they had forged. The crisis had been averted, but the journey had left its mark on each of them. As they looked at the new Origin Tree and the girl who now carried its legacy, they knew that this was only the beginning of a new chapter for the realm of Echoes.

With their mission successful and their adventure ending in success, Alex and his friends began their journey back to the capital, the atmosphere much lighter than before. The path seemed brighter, the air fresher, as if the land itself was celebrating their victory. As they approached the city gates, Master Shoi and several other masters were there to greet them.

"Welcome back," Master Shoi said, his face breaking into a wide smile. "Congratulations on saving the world."

Alex nodded, his own smile mirroring Shoi's. "It wasn't easy, but we did it together," he replied.

Master Shoi placed a hand on Alex's shoulder. "You should eventually be able to return to your own world, but if you decide to stay here, you are welcome to do so."

Alex glanced at his friends, the bonds they had formed over their adventures strengthening his resolve. "I think I'll stay here a little while longer," he said, looking at Elara, Luna, Theron, Eirys, and Dracy. "I've found new friends and new reasons to stay."

After a warm conversation with Master Shoi and the other masters, Alex and the others decided to grab a meal at Uncle Drago's Restaurant. It had become a tradition of sorts, a way to celebrate their victories and cherish their time together.

As they entered the bustling restaurant, Alex turned to Dracy, a playful glint in his eyes. "This time, I'm going to try every dish they serve."

Dracy laughed, her excitement contagious. "I'm more excited to have Elara try their dumplings. I love their dumplings!"

They sat down at a large table, the familiar aromas of Uncle Drago's cooking enveloping them. Plates of food were brought out, each dish more delicious than the last. Laughter and conversation filled the air as they shared stories and enjoyed their meal.

Elara took a bite of a dumpling, her eyes widening in delight. "These are amazing!" she exclaimed, her face lighting up with a smile.

Dracy beamed with pride. "I knew you'd love them!"

As they continued their feast, Alex looked around the table at his friends, feeling a deep sense of gratitude. They had faced countless challenges and emerged stronger together. The journey had been long and arduous, but it had also been filled with moments of joy and camaraderie.

They sat together, enjoying their meal and each other's company, rekindling their friendship for another adventure. The realm of Echoes had been saved, and now, they could look forward to the future with hope and excitement.

Milton Keynes UK
Ingram Content Group UK Ltd.
UKHW020842180924
448440UK00002B/3

9 798330 393527